D0455102

Also by Kevin van Whye

Date Me, Bryson Keller

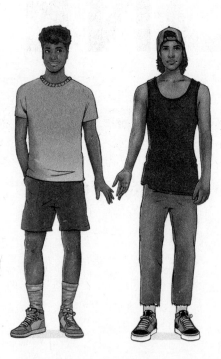

NATE
plus
ONE

WITHDRAWN

Kevin van Whye

Random House New York

This is a work of fiction. Names, characters, places, and incidents either are the product of the author's imagination or are used fictitiously. Any resemblance to actual persons, living or dead, events, or locales is entirely coincidental.

Text copyright © 2022 by Kevin van Whye
Jacket art copyright © 2022 by Kingsley Nebechi

All rights reserved. Published in the United States by Random House Children's Books, a division of Penguin Random House LLC, New York.

Random House and the colophon are registered trademarks of Penguin Random House LLC.

Visit us on the Web! GetUnderlined.com

Educators and librarians, for a variety of teaching tools, visit us at RHTeachersLibrarians.com

Library of Congress Cataloging-in-Publication Data is available upon request.
ISBN 978-0-593-37642-3 (hardcover) | ISBN 978-0-593-37643-0 (lib. bdg.) | ISBN 978-0-593-37644-7 (ebook)

Printed in the United States of America
10 9 8 7 6 5 4 3 2 1
First Edition

Random House Children's Books supports the First Amendment and celebrates the right to read.

Penguin Random House LLC supports copyright. Copyright fuels creativity, encourages diverse voices, promotes free speech, and creates a vibrant culture. Thank you for buying an authorized edition of this book and for complying with copyright laws by not reproducing, scanning, or distributing any part in any form without permission. You are supporting writers and allowing Penguin Random House to publish books for every reader.

To my family, for always being in my corner

1

Jai Patel looks sexy when he is onstage.

Or in this case, standing in Lauren Hall's living room and plucking the strings of his guitar to one of the Weeknd's songs. It's Saturday night, and we're at Lauren's house for her birthday party, which is always the event of the year.

Jai's band, Infinite Sorrow, gathers around him as the lead singer, Ross Sherman, belts out the song that has been overplayed on the radio these past few months. Infinite Sorrow is great, as always, but tonight my eyes are only on Jai.

His black, shoulder-length hair is down, and he's wearing a T-shirt with ripped sleeves and skinny black jeans, also ripped. Sweat coats his warm brown skin as he sways to the rhythm of the song.

"If you stare any harder, Nate, Jai will be permanently burned into your retinas," whispers Gemma Roth, one of my two best friends. She is an aspiring fashion designer, and this party has provided her with the perfect opportunity to showcase her work. She's wearing a two-color jumpsuit that stands out against her pale skin. The front is red, the back black. Her ink-black hair is tied into a bun, revealing her ears and eight piercings—five in her right, three in her left.

My jeans and Final Fantasy T-shirt pale in comparison to Gemma's well-thought-out, flashy outfit. Some people are born for the spotlight, like Gemma and Jai, whereas I'm more of a behind-the-scenes kind of guy. It's why I dream of being a songwriter instead of a singer.

"This is me just supporting my best friend and his band," I whisper back with a wink. "It's totally innocent staring."

Maybe in the past Gemma would have believed me, but we both know that Jai also happens to be a boy who, more and more, is starting to make me feel certain *things*. It wasn't always like this. At first he was simply a friend—a close one. But over time my feelings have grown into something more.

I can say with certainty that I have a crush on Jai.

"Sure," Gemma says. "And I'm secretly a princess who will be swept off to a fictional European country by my posh estranged grandmother." Gemma made me binge-watch most of Anne Hathaway's filmography over one weekend last summer, which of course included *The Princess Diaries*. Ever since Gemma discovered the old but never-out-of-style masterpiece that is *The Devil Wears Prada*, Anne Hathaway has become her favorite actor. She has seen the movie more times than I can count. It should be noted that "Anne's very unsupportive boyfriend was and will always be trash." Gemma's words, not mine.

"Here," Gemma says. She hands me one of the two red Solo cups that she's holding. I take a sip. The beer is warm and sour. I've never been much of a drinker, and I skipped Lauren's party last year because *he'd* been too busy to go.

I take a large gulp of beer to chase away the bitter memories. I would rather not spend my night thinking of *him*. In my haste, I swallow hard and end up choking.

"Easy there, tiger." Gemma pats me on the back. "We have work tomorrow, remember?"

I shoot her a death glare. "I was all for skipping tonight," I remind her. "You wanted to come."

"And aren't you happy you did?" Gemma says. She tilts her head toward Jai, in the throes of the song he's playing. "You would have missed this."

Touché.

Gemma rests a hand on my shoulder. "You know, a crush stays a crush unless you actively do something about it."

I can't say anything to that. And I don't need to, because judging by the knowing smirk on Gemma's crimson lips, she understands she's won. Sometimes best friends are insufferable.

Just after midnight, Infinite Sorrow finishes their set, and they leave the makeshift stage behind. I'm standing alone with my still-half-full cup (or is it half-empty?) of even warmer beer. Gemma has disappeared to be the social butterfly that she is, leaving me to peacefully ogle Jai.

I mean, the band. I was totally listening to the music.

Jai walks up to me. He runs a hand through his sweat-dampened hair and smiles.

"How are we?" he asks. He sounds so happy, so satisfied, that it makes me smile too.

"Fantastic," I say. "As always."

"You're biased," Jai teases. It's true, but not for the reasons

3

he's thinking. Of course, I'm still a massive fan of the band. But now I'm an even bigger fan of Jai Patel.

Jai peers down at my cup. "Are you going to finish that?" I hold it out to him. "Thanks," he says.

I watch as he brings the cup to his lips and takes a slow sip. The fact that my lips touched that very cup moments ago is almost too much for me to handle.

God, teenage hormones are wild AF.

Ross comes over to us, holding his own Solo cup. He's rolled up the sleeves of his T-shirt and is showing off his toned arms. According to some fans of Infinite Sorrow, Ross should be the sole object of fangirl desire. I mean, I can't argue with that. With his curly black hair and piercing blue eyes, he *is* attractive.

But he still does not compare to Jai Patel. And I will be hearing no further arguments on that matter—looking at you, @IloveRoss1—thank you very much.

Ross pulls Jai into a hushed conversation, and I check my phone to avoid eavesdropping. Mom sent a text telling me she's on her way to pick me up. We agreed that I would stay until she punched out at midnight. With Jai's performance over, I can't say that I have any desire to linger at the party.

Jai laughs at something Ross says, which draws my attention to them. They're standing close together. Very buddy-buddy. Sometimes—and I know this is really petty of me—I'm jealous of Ross, that he shares something with Jai that I don't. As a fan and not a member of Infinite Sorrow, I will always be on the outside looking in.

You had your chance, a bitter thought reminds me. And it's true.

Before Ross was chosen as the lead singer of Infinite Sorrow, Jai had offered me the chance to audition. He knew I could sing and that I was a fan of their songs. And while a part of me did want to try out, I flashed back to the time I was twelve years old and Mom let me go to music camp.

All the campers had to audition for the end-of-summer performance, and of course I was eager to try out just like everyone else. I vividly recall standing onstage the day of the audition. Everyone's eyes were on me, and when I opened my mouth to sing, I couldn't produce a single sound. I just stood there, moving my lips in silence like a fish in a tank. That was the birth of my stage fright.

Five years later, I have yet to set foot on another stage.

I spot Gemma across the living room and head over to her. She's socializing with Alice Wu and Monique Thompson, two of her fellow debate club members. It's the one club Gemma joined not simply to boost her college applications but because she actually liked it. She's now one of the most valued members of Wychwood High's team.

"Mom says she's on her way," I tell Gemma. We've planned to drop off Gemma at her home.

"Give me five," Gemma says. "I really need the bathroom."

"I'll be outside," I tell her.

I leave the still-busy space and maneuver my way to the front door. Given the number of people at the party, it takes me longer than it should to finally make it outside. The warm night greets me, and I'm happy to leave the smell of sweat, booze, and hormones behind. I fill my lungs with the fresh, salty air of late spring.

I pull out my phone, and I'm scrolling through Instagram when I feel someone standing next to me. I turn, half expecting it to be Gemma, but it's not her. It's Jai.

"There you are," Jai says, and he almost sounds relieved. "I thought you'd left already."

I shake my head. "Not yet. I just went to tell Gemma that Mom's on her way over."

"I'm going to get the band stuff loaded and call it a night too," Jai says. Our eyes meet. "Are you working tomorrow?"

I nod. "Yeah. Gemma and I have a shift."

"Cool," Jai says. "I'll swing by the diner then." He smiles and turns to head back inside the house.

Weird.

As I watch him step across the threshold, I swallow the desire to tell him that we have school on Monday and he should take it easy tomorrow instead of coming to the diner. Because the truth is that I want to see him. And the promise that I *will* draws a smile on my face.

I like Jai more and more with each passing day. It's one of those things that are hard to explain but just happen, like how sometimes it rains when the sun's still shining or how you can laugh until you cry. Small everyday miracles.

And the more I think about it, even liking Jai Patel was totally accidental. It was totally unavoidable too.

2

Big Mo's Diner is where I spend most of my weekends—working. The sizzling of burgers, the shuffling of feet, and the clanging of cutlery are the soundtrack to my shift. Big Mo's is busy any day that ends in a *y*, and Sunday is no different. We're just now starting to see the lull after the evening crowd.

"Can I get two number two specials with a large strawberry milkshake and one cola, please?" I ask the cook and co-owner, Retta Jones.

"You got it, Nathan," Retta calls back.

Gemma sidles up to me. She's carrying an empty tray and wearing the green apron that's part of our uniform.

"Looks like Brody's got a new girlfriend . . . again," Gemma says with an exasperated sigh. "It's Kate from history."

Brody Miller is the quarterback of Wychwood High's very own Titans. With his blond hair, blue eyes, and yearlong summer body, Brody is desired by many at school. I was one of them as a freshman—Gemma was too, in sophomore year.

"Really? Kate." I shake my head. "How many does that make?"

Gemma shrugs. "You would think that by now people would stop falling for his BS."

"The allure of popularity is intoxicating," I say. "Dating Brody Miller automatically makes you part of the 'it' couple. So are they 'Brate' or 'Krody'?"

"They should be 'Barf,'" Gemma says. "For the record, couple names are disgusting and I hate them." She turns to me. "Anyway, who has the time for that when we have dreams to chase? In a few months we'll all be seniors. The pressure is on." Ever since Gemma stumbled across her older sister watching a marathon of *Project Runway*, she's wanted to walk the halls of Parsons School of Design in New York City.

It really does feel like our whole lives depend on this moment and which school we get into. Our dreams are on the line, so I understand the pressure. Fashion school has been Gemma's goal for so long, and I want this for her. Even if it means we end up on opposite sides of the country.

"Here you go, Nate. Two number twos, strawberry milkshake, and one cola," Retta says.

"Thanks." I load my tray and carefully make my way to the diners. "Here you go, Mr. and Mrs. Grant."

"Thank you so much, Nathan," Mrs. Grant says.

Big Mo's Diner is south of Main Street in Wychwood, which is located just west of San Diego. It is a town trying to be a city but failing, and everyone knows everyone.

"Enjoy your meal," I say. I head back to the counter. There are three other servers besides Gemma and me. The two of us are the only part-timers, though. We got the jobs after Big Mo's was featured on a show on the Food Network, which turned the diner into the number one hub for everyone who calls Wychwood home and those just passing through. Big Mo is short for Big Moses, the very big man who co-owns the place. His imposing stature made him a rising star in college basketball, but an injury prevented him from going pro. It did not, however, hurt his jovial temperament.

Mom and Retta have been best friends since college. When Retta asked if I'd be interested in working part-time, I jumped at the chance. I also asked if there was an opening for Gemma. That was before Jai moved to town and our friend group became a party of three. Gemma and I have been working the weekend shifts ever since.

With most of the booths empty now, I busy myself with finishing my biology homework before closing. I need to figure out which genes a make-believe baby will inherit from its make-believe parents. The fact that Ms. Crowley is still giving us homework when most of us have already switched into summer break mode is a travesty of justice.

Brody and Kate sit in the corner booth, huddled close together with smiles on their faces. For a moment I feel jealous. I didn't get to do any of that with my ex.

I will not lose myself going down memory lane. I will not think of *him*. I turn my focus back to completing my homework, and ten minutes later it's finished.

I start to wipe down my tables, when Gemma snaps her fingers to get my attention.

"Retta says we can leave when we're done." There's still twenty minutes before closing, but Retta lets us leave early once the evening crowd is on its way out.

"I'll tell my mom," I say.

"You haven't checked your phone, have you?" Gemma asks.

"No, why?" I stop wiping down the table and pull out my phone. There are two unread messages in our group chat.

I'm around. I'll give you guys a ride home.

The message is from Jai. I guess he's keeping his word and swinging by. I can't help but smile.

We're still cleaning up when the bell above the door announces Jai's arrival. He's wearing a cap on backward, a T-shirt with a picture of a surfboard on it, cutoff jeans, and sneakers. He looks every bit like the resident of a coastal town.

Jai folds his lanky frame into one of the booths. He scratches his chin, and I take him all in. My eyes move from his sharp jaw to his proud nose and to his lips, which I wish would meet mine. . . . I shake my head. Now is not the time for this. I'm in public, for heaven's sake.

"Hey, Gem, hey, Nate," Jai says, and his warm smile makes my heart skip a beat.

"Hey, we're almost done here," Gemma tells him.

"No problem. I can wait."

"You want anything?" I ask. My face still feels flushed.

"Coffee," Jai says. I get him a cup and sit opposite him. Up close I notice that his clothes are wet. Jai removes his cap and runs a hand through his hair.

"Is it raining?" I ask. He clearly isn't dressed for this weather.

"Yeah. Just came out of nowhere," Jai replies. He holds the cup of coffee to his lips and looks at me through the steam.

By the time we exit Big Mo's, it's no longer just a light shower. It's downpour-adjacent.

"Well, crap, we're going to get soaked," Gemma says. "I just finished sewing this jacket." She sourced this vintage denim piece from her favorite thrift shop. Most of Gemma's clothes are either originals or secondhand finds that she's revamped and personalized.

"We'll have to make a run for it," Jai says. "On three." He looks at us and winks. "One, two . . ."

Before he gets to the last number, he starts sprinting through the rain. I brace myself for the cool spring shower and dash after him. Gemma follows with a squeal. By the time we reach Jai's car, I'm pretty sure all three of us are soaked to our underwear.

Jai drives an old VW minibus—the kind that screams hippie but also perfectly suits beachside towns like Wychwood. It may be odd to see a high school student driving this car, but it makes sense for Jai because it's big enough for carting his band equipment around.

Gemma climbs into the back. Her house is closest to Big Mo's, so we usually drop her off first.

"It's really coming down now." Gemma holds out her hand and catches a few drops.

For a moment we just sit and watch the rain fall all around us. Jai removes his cap and uses the hair tie on his wrist to pull his hair into a loose knot—and now I'm not watching the rain anymore. When he catches me looking, I turn away quickly. A smile tugs at his lips.

Jai reaches to the seat next to Gemma and hands out towels.

"They're clean," Jai assures us. "I was going to hit the pool tonight, but the rain has kind of put an end to that plan."

Jai used to be a competitive swimmer. But he was forced

to quit because of an injury, which is one of the reasons he transferred to Wychwood High. Jai Patel was once the star of an überprestigious school called Fairvale Academy, about two hours away. He had a swimming scholarship to boot. After a car accident and his parents' divorce, Jai's family moved from Fairvale to Wychwood for his mom's work. He still swims for fun and exercise.

I catch sight of myself in the rearview mirror. My hair has a habit of turning into a frizzy ball of fluff whenever it's wet, and my decision to keep it just a bit longer than usual makes it look all that much worse. I groan.

"Cute," Jai says.

"What?" I think I've misheard him. Instead of repeating himself, Jai smiles and starts the engine. Soon we're pulling out of Big Mo's parking lot.

Gemma's house is a five-minute drive from the diner, so we drop her off pronto. We park in the driveway and watch as she makes a mad dash for the front door. She shrieks with every step.

As Jai backs up, I connect his iPod to the car's audio and hit play. It takes me a moment to recognize Jai's voice.

"I want to run / Get away faster than you can catch me / I want to run / Far away, where no one can tame me / Run, run (run away) / Live my life on the run / I'm chasing my dreams and no one can stop me / So I'll run."

"What's this?" I ask.

"Just something I've been working on," Jai says.

"For Ready2Rock?"

Ready2Rock is an annual competition for indie bands held

in LA. Anyone can enter, but only ten bands make it to the final and get a chance to perform live. This year, the contest is in partnership with Ezra Grace, the lead singer of the Graces. The champions will not only get a chance to open for them but also get ten grand. Winning can be a band's big break. After doing well in the online preliminary rounds, Infinite Sorrow has made it to the live final, and fans think they stand a good chance of becoming champions. According to the comments online, Infinite Sorrow and another band, Thorn, are the front-runners.

"No," Jai says. "We're all set for that."

"I hope you guys win." I want them to crush it, not only because I'm Jai's friend but also because I'm a fan of the band.

"Me too," Jai says.

My apartment isn't far from Big Mo's, which is another reason I enjoy working there. Soon after Jai's song stops playing, Jai pulls into the building's parking lot and idles just before the entrance.

I turn to him. "Thanks for the ride."

"No problem," Jai says.

My eyes snag on his lips. Jai catches me looking, and our eyes lock. I start to fiddle with a loose thread on my T-shirt to distract myself.

"Uh, see ya," I say, breaking the growing silence. I climb from his car and head for the door.

I don't want Jai to know how I feel about him.

I can't help but replay Gemma's words from last night: *"A crush stays a crush unless you actively do something about it."*

Yeah, yeah, yeah. Easier said than done.

3

The invitation to my cousin's wedding in South Africa arrives two weeks before summer break. That's two weeks before we're set to fly out. The once-white envelope is now stained yellow, and the edges are crinkled and somewhat damaged. A collection of postmarks from its European detour covers the front, along with REBECCA AND NATHAN HARGREAVES in silver calligraphy.

"Mom, look what finally came," I say as I enter the front door. It's Monday after school, and Jai just dropped me off at home.

Our apartment is small, but it's fine for just the two of us. There are two bedrooms and even two bathrooms, so Mom and I never have to share. Which helps, because on a good day Mom takes an hour in the bathroom just to get ready, even though she wears a uniform to work.

Both Mom and I are pretty bad at checking our mailbox. So much so that I've taken to setting a reminder on my phone every week to do the task. In the past, our upstairs neighbor—and

Mom's nemesis—Mr. Schuster has complained that our mailbox is unsightly because of all the letters sticking out. It's one of his numerous complaints about us, according to our super. So we've been in a cold war with Mr. Schuster for the last two years. And he loves to use every excuse he has to come and knock on the door to whine. I have a theory that he's in love with Mom and that's why he's always in our business. Either that or he's racist. It's a fifty-fifty chance.

Mom's on the couch with her feet up and her eyes closed. She's still in her nurse scrubs, which are embroidered with the Wychwood Memorial logo.

"Hey, Sonno."

Sonno is the nickname my dad had for me. He was from South Africa, and apparently it's a common term of endearment there. I don't remember much about him. And the memories I do have of him have slowly faded with time. "Dad" is a word I know but never learned the real meaning of.

Dad died when I was five years old. It's not like I resent him or anything. After all, dying wasn't his choice. Car accidents happen without our say-so. In my head I know that Dad didn't choose to die, but all my heart knows is that I miss him.

With Dad gone, Mom took over. She still has clear memories of him. I hear her cry when she looks at our photo albums from time to time. While it hurts me to have so few memories of Dad, it's apparent that the alternative—remembering too much—is also painful.

"You just get back?" I ask.

"Yeah. What a day." Mom lets out a groan as she scoots

over to make room for me on the couch, where I throw myself down and stretch my legs out. Mom and I are about the same height and build, tall and lanky.

Mom leans in to read the invitation over my shoulder. She runs a hand over the gold foil detail and then whistles. "Fancy. Of course, Sylvia is going big for the wedding."

"I'm not complaining," I say. "We're getting a free flight to South Africa."

It'll be my first time ever going to South Africa, and my first time meeting a lot of that side of the family—my dad's side. Mom and I will be staying with my grandmother, which I'm excited about because she's my only living grandparent. The last time I saw her, I was going through puberty, and I was a moody mess of pimples and hormones. Since then I've only ever seen her through Skype and heard her voice over the phone every few months.

Of all my extended family, I've spent the most time with Aunt Sylvia and Meghan—the wife and daughter of Dad's older brother. They frequent the States. Meghan is studying business at Stanford. She is the heir to a hotel conglomerate, after all.

But when I think of Stanford, I don't think of my cousin. I think of *him*. He's a freshman there this year. Though I haven't heard from him since early last summer.

"It even feels expensive," I say to shake my memories of *him*. I rub my finger over the broken wax seal. Despite its current state, it's clear that this piece of paper carries a hefty price.

"Sylvia probably spent as much as I earn in a month on the invitations alone."

"Lifestyles of the filthy rich," I say.

"I'm just glad I have enough money to send you to college," Mom says. The USC Thornton School of Music has been my dream school for so long that I'm a ball of nerves whenever I think of applying next year. I need to pass the audition and earn my spot. *I have to.*

"You'll get in, Sonno," Mom says. "I believe in you." It's as if she knows just what I'm thinking. Sometimes Mom knows me better than I know myself. It's what made coming out to her feel more like a duet than a solo performance.

Mom runs her hand through her curly brown hair, which is similar to mine. Genes, I guess. Everyone says I look like her because we have the same warm brown skin with dark hair and eyes. Mom is mixed race and so was my dad, so of course I am too. I'm not sure exactly which side of the family I look more like, but according to Mom, I have my dad's nose and smile. I also inherited his love of and knack for music.

"I can't believe we're finally getting a stamp on our passports," I say, my face gleaming.

"You're really excited, huh?" Mom says.

"Yeah. Very. Though I'm also kind of nervous," I admit. This event will be the first time I see my extended family since coming out. Hell, it will be my first time seeing some of them, period. So I am more than a little nervous, but I know that having Mom by my side will make a world of difference. I'm lucky to have someone as amazing and supportive as she is in my life—not every gay kid gets this. And I'll need the support at the wedding.

Apparently, an Instagram post I made after coming out

last fall made a splash in one of the family WhatsApp groups. Meghan said her mom shut down any and all homophobic comments from Dad's cousins in the chat. Ever since I first heard about the wedding from Aunt Sylvia, facing them has been one of my fears. But of all my family members, I'm most nervous to see Uncle Richard, Dad's only brother. We haven't really talked since I came out. Uncle Richard is my closest link to Dad, and I'm not sure if my coming out has changed that.

"You'll be fine," Mom says as she gets up from the sofa and walks to the kitchen. "Just have fun." She opens the fridge door. "We have leftover chow mein. Do you want some?"

"No, thanks. I grabbed something to eat with Gemma." I roll off the couch and head to my room.

I wouldn't say that I'm a neat freak, but I do believe that everything has its place—except the mail, of course. But really, few sights make me angrier than stuff being where it doesn't belong. And I mean Hulk-level angry.

My bedroom walls are mostly covered in video game posters. A TV and a gaming console stand before my much-loved and well-used lime-green beanbag chair. And on the other side of my bedroom sit a keyboard and a guitar.

I plug the charger into my dead phone and head to the bathroom. I get under the water and begin my live shower concert.

"*I'm not trying to save you / I'm just trying to save me.*" I start to sing "Antihero." It's one of Infinite Sorrow's songs that I love. I knew it even before I met and became friends with Jai. It still amazes me that *he* wrote this song, which so perfectly speaks to me.

"*I'm not trying to save you / I'm just trying to save me / Got nothin' to lose / Got my life to gain / This is me, the hero of my own story / But you might not see it that way, and I don't care."*

The lyrics are about a person living their life on their terms, even if it means being viewed as an antihero by society. Jai told me he had written the song while coming to terms with being bi.

Truth be told, I was lucky not to fear coming out to Mom. And yet, just before I told her that I was gay, I had a brief meltdown, because coming out is such a huge moment in a teenager's life. Times may have changed, but the feeling you get when you step out of the closet hasn't. Unless we start asking straight people to come out too, this norm needs to go. Seriously, who said that's the norm?

After my shower, I throw myself into bed and look at the photo that hangs on the wall across from me. It's four-year-old me sitting on Dad's shoulders at a picnic. He and I are wearing matching red plaid shirts. It's the last photo ever taken of us together. It's one more lost memory of him.

Dad is another big reason why I'm excited about this trip.

I've never said this to Mom, but I wonder if she knows. Sure, a lavish party sounds fun. But the idea of setting foot where Dad stood, of visiting his home, is what I'm really looking forward to.

I keep my questions and thoughts about Dad locked up in this secret compartment in my heart. This wedding feels like the right time to open it.

4

I wake up on Tuesday morning to an ominous sight. Beyoncé is dead.

No, not *that* Beyoncé. I mean the pet goldfish that Jai got me for my birthday last year. He said that if I were an animal, I'd probably be a goldfish because of my bad memory. Seriously, I'm always forgetting things and need to write them down. The problem is I forget where I put those reminders too.

I'm staring at Beyoncé lying belly-up in her tank. I pick her up by the tail and carry her to the bathroom. With a remorseful sigh, I flush the toilet, sending my pet to the afterlife . . . or rather, to Wychwood's interconnected sewage system.

As much as I want to, I don't have time to mourn, because every morning is a scramble for Mom and me.

I'm pulling on a pair of black jeans when Mom shouts from the living room. "Have you seen my keys?" Anyone who knows me and meets Mom knows where I get my forgetfulness from.

"Did you check your jacket from yesterday?" I call.

I throw on a white T-shirt with a PlayStation buttons graphic. I'm sitting on my bed, tying the shoelaces on my Jordans, when Mom shouts back, "Found them!"

I grab my backpack and find Mom standing at the door tying her hair. "Are you ready? Let's go!"

Most days we barely manage to arrive at school on time going the speed limit, and today is no different. As Mom races way over what's legal, I hold on tight and pray that we don't die.

Or get another speeding ticket to add to Mom's growing collection.

Mom drops me off in the parking lot of Wychwood High, and I rush to say goodbye before the bell rings. I run like the wind, managing to make it on time to first period.

History is next, and as usual, I sit beside Gemma.

"Was it down to the wire again?" she asks.

"You know my mom." I nod.

"You could ask Jai for a ride," Gemma says. "I'm sure he wouldn't mind."

I shake my head. Jai has offered before—numerous times—but I've always turned him down because he and I live on opposite sides of Wychwood, so it would be a massive inconvenience. It's fine on occasion, but getting a ride every day would be too much.

Kate saunters in as if she's walking on literal clouds. I spy Brody at the door. It seems he's walked her to class. Kate takes her seat and immediately checks her phone with a huge grin on her face. I *know* that smile. It's the "I just got a text from someone I like" smile.

Brody is still at the doorway with, big shocker, his phone in his hand. Call me bitter, but this seems like overkill.

You were just like that when you were dating, a small voice in my head reminds me. And as much as I hate to admit it, it's true. I *was* just like that. I still remember those exact emotions. I went through it all. The texting and the flirting. The wonderful whirlwind of courting. I lived this with *him*—the son of Satan! That's maybe a little dramatic, but he lost the right to even be named.

And yet I still miss it from time to time.

I have all of his text messages saved, which is a painful confession to make. I may be ready to move on . . . but I haven't just yet. Baby steps. Forgetting first loves is a complicated and messy affair.

Our history teacher, Mr. Ellis, continues his review in preparation for finals. I focus on taking notes, and history class passes by in a blur.

"I have a club meeting at lunch," Gemma reminds me when the bell rings.

Gemma has always loved school activities, and I never have. We're total opposites, but it's always been us against the world. We met the first day of kindergarten, and more than a decade later we're still going strong. When Jai first transferred to the school and we became friends, our dynamic definitely changed, which took some getting used to. Gemma and I have fought. And there was even that very dark period in eighth grade when we didn't talk to each other for almost two weeks. We don't speak of that terrible time, but we survived it.

Before Jai, whenever Gemma had a meeting, it meant I'd have to eat alone. But I always have someone to sit with now.

"I'll see you later." Gemma peaces out.

I nod and we head in opposite directions. Jai and I have next period together: biology with Ms. Crowley. The class is always tough to endure, but today it promises to be insufferable.

"I know summer break's just around the corner. But let's mix things up and swap seat partners," Ms. Crowley announces. She looks delighted by the idea, and her smile only grows when she hears several of us groan.

I frown. Is this even a thing? I am one of the groaners, because there are a few homophobic asshats that I would rather not be seated next to for the last couple weeks of the school year. See: Montgomery Welsh.

My coming out was mostly fine, save for Montgomery and his bullshit. Some people are walking high school clichés, and he is one of them. It's thanks to those clichés that I know Montgomery is *that* boy who peaks in high school. And it thrills me to know that in five years or less, all his hate and bigotry will have come back to bite him in his ass.

"Everyone, gather your things and come to the front of the class." We do. I mean, we have no real say in the matter. I stand toward the back and wait for my name to be called. Jai joins me.

"I swear she treats us like little kids," Jai whispers, and I nod. We've been subjected to Ms. Crowley's whims all year.

"Gemma has a club meeting at lunch," I whisper. I'm super close to Jai, so our conversation goes undetected.

"It'll just be the two of us, then." He winks, and I smile at the prospect of us being alone. I'm the first to look away.

I notice then that there are only six students waiting to be seated. When Montgomery is paired with Lia Thorpe, I thank the universe for its favor.

"Nathan," Ms. Crowley calls. "You'll be sitting with Jai."

Thank you, Ms. Crowley, for this wonderful idea. You deserve the world!

"Nice," Jai says as we sit on our lab stools.

Our knees touch. I stop breathing for a hot minute, before exhaling through my front teeth. Jai is unaware of the effect he has on me.

Ms. Crowley starts to drone on about the Human Genome Project, and I lose interest fast. Instead I line a page in my notebook and start to scribble down a melody, all while stealing a few glances at Jai—just a few.

The bell rings, and I stand to collect my things. Jai stays seated, staring at his phone screen. He hunches his shoulders and furrows his brow.

"What's wrong?" I ask.

Without saying anything, he hands me his phone. It's open on Ross's Instagram, and he's shared a post from Thorn, Infinite Sorrow's rival band. Thorn is announcing their new member—and it's Ross.

This doesn't make any sense. Ross is the lead singer of Infinite Sorrow. He just performed with them this weekend!

Everything suddenly seems to click for Jai. The shock on his face wears off, and he wastes no time. He's out of his seat.

I want to say something, but it's too late. I grab my things and chase after him, still holding his phone in my hand.

Crowds of teens start to fill the hallways, and I fall farther behind.

By the time I catch up to Jai, he and Ross are already staring each other down. Liam, the drummer with Infinite Sorrow, is standing between them, holding a hand against Jai's chest.

"What the hell is going on?" Jai asks.

Tension fills the air like a gas leak. Just a spark and everything will explode. Everyone around must feel it too, because they're all gathered there, waiting and watching.

"I guess the news is out," Ross says. "Look, I wanted to tell you, but everything happened so fast that I couldn't."

"How could you do this?" Liam interjects. "This is low of you, Ross."

Ross turns to Liam. "Stay out of this."

"If you really wanted to tell me, you would have," Jai says. His eyes are filled with hurt and anger. But it seems the latter is winning. "You should have at least given me a warning. You know how important this competition is."

"Of course I know," Ross says. "It's the opportunity of a lifetime. It means the world to me too, which is why I couldn't say no to this."

"We could have made it together—that was our plan," Jai says. "Is it because we didn't sing one of your songs?"

Ross rolls his eyes. "This is business, Jai. Nothing personal. With Thorn, I can be the star. You think I like always being in your shadow? If I stayed, that's exactly what would happen.

You're the sun and we're all just revolving around you. You're always the one making decisions. This song. This tempo. This key. It's always you, you, you."

"You should have told me this is how you feel," Jai says. "You never said anything."

"You didn't notice because you don't need to, not when you're the center," Ross says. "Infinite Sorrow will survive as long as it has you."

"That isn't true," Jai argues. "The band is for all of us. It *is* all of us." Jai searches his friend's face. "Is this about your ego? Is that why you screwed us over?"

"No, this is about my potential," Ross states. "You have never valued it. Thorn does. They are going places. I'm going places."

Jai's eyes spew only anger, no more sadness.

"This is such bullshit," Liam spits. "The final is just over a month away. What are we supposed to do?"

"That's not my problem," Ross says. "But good luck. I think you're going to really need it."

What an asshole, I think. I notice Jai is clenching his fist. He looks like he's half a breath away from painting these gray hallways crimson. Go, Titans?

I reach out and grab Jai's arm just as he's making a move toward Ross, whose eyes widen with fear. Jai looks at me and stills.

"Later." Ross turns on his heel and pushes through the crowd.

Jai releases an audible sigh. His fists are still clenched, but his face softens as anger leaves his body. I realize I'm still holding on to him. I let him go just as fast as I reached for him.

Jai storms off, not saying a word. Liam and I share a look and chase after him. Without a lead singer Infinite Sorrow's chances of winning Ready2Rock are dead on arrival. We find Jai on the steps leading out to the parking lot.

"Are you okay?" I ask, even though he clearly isn't. But I don't know what else to say or do. I am probably the most awkward when it comes to comforting people.

"Yes," Jai says, but then he sighs. "No." Our eyes meet. "Maybe?"

"I can't believe that asshole," Liam says.

"You have to win," I say. "You have to beat Thorn."

They look at me. It's Jai who speaks. "That's going to be really hard to do, because we currently don't have a lead singer."

"You can sing, Jai," Liam says.

"As backup. I don't sing lead." I can hear the frustration in Jai's voice.

"Or we can hold auditions." Liam sounds panicked. This is an emergency.

"Ready2Rock is next month. There isn't much time. There's no way a new singer will be prepared." Jai closes his eyes. As his friend, I know how much this means to him. He and Infinite Sorrow have been working toward the final for six months, and in one move Ross has blown all of that up. It's unfair and it sucks.

So then I make a move that's completely unexpected, even by me. Maybe it's because I know how much this opportunity means to Jai. And I support him and his dream, not just because I like him, but because he's a friend. Or maybe it's simply that I want to use this chance to finally conquer my stage fright. Whatever the reason is, I clear my throat and say, "There is a singer who already knows all your songs."

"Who?" Liam asks.

Jai looks at me. I see the hope dawn on his face when he realizes what I mean. Even though the thought of singing onstage fills me with dread, I smile when I say, "Me."

5

"You sing?" Liam sounds surprised. The only people who have ever heard me sing are Mom, Gemma, and Jai. My stage fright has firmly kept my voice silent.

"Are you sure?" Jai looks at me.

I nod.

"I guess crisis averted, then." Liam smiles, and his freckles bunch up on his cheeks. "So . . . we're still on for practice today?"

"Sure," Jai says before turning to me. "We should talk."

Liam looks between the two of us. He knows he's missing something. "Well then, uh . . . I'll see you guys later," he says, and walks away.

"You don't need to do this," Jai starts. "You don't need to force yourself."

"I want to do this. I *need* to do this. You know the Thornton School of Music is my dream. I have to audition as part of my application. This seems like a good opportunity to deal with my stage fright." I can see the concern in his eyes. "Of course, I also really want to help you and the band."

Jai is quiet for a while. Then he says, "Are you free after school? We have practice."

Diving right into the deep end—oh boy.

"Yeah," I say. "I'll just text my mom a heads-up."

Grrr. My stomach chooses that moment to announce that it is empty. Breakfast isn't really something we do in my house, because we're always rushing. Skipping breakfast hasn't always been by choice, but now my body has adapted to the habit.

"How about Big Mo's for lunch?" Jai asks. "I could use a break from this place."

I nod. "Sounds good." We walk toward Jai's car, and I finally hand him back his phone.

As usual, Big Mo's is busy. "Hey, Nate," Lucille, one of the regular servers, says as she passes by with a plate of fries. The smell makes my stomach growl again.

Jai laughs. "You must be really hungry."

"Understatement," I say as we slide into an empty booth. I shift in my seat and move my legs, but Jai's are just as long as mine, so it seems impossible. In the end, I give up and our knees touch. Not that I'm complaining about it.

"What can I get you boys?" Lucille asks.

"Cheeseburger and fries, please," I say.

"Make that two," Jai adds. He holds up two fingers, one of which sports a ring.

"Anything to drink?"

At the exact same time we both say, "Sprite." Our love of

30

Sprite is another thing that I have in common with Jai. Before him, Gemma always mocked my drink of choice, claiming it was strange that I ordered "glorified water with fizz" instead of Coke.

Lucille leaves to grab our drinks, and I turn to find Jai staring at me. "What is it?" I ask.

"Thank you," he says.

"For what?"

"For just now. Volunteering to sing with us." He smiles.

"No problem. I know how much this means to you. And to the rest of the band," I say.

"Still. I owe you. Big-time."

"You don't. We're not bartering here," I say. "Though I wouldn't say no to you buying me fries after every rehearsal. You know how much I love Big Mo's fries!"

Jai laughs. "I could do that, but what would I owe you after the performance?"

"A very, very large order," I say.

"Deal."

"I'm joking," I say. "You don't need to do anything for me. We're friends."

"Right. Friends." But the way he says it sounds weird—loaded somehow. Am I reading too much into it?

Before I can question it out loud, Lucille returns with our food, some cutlery, and napkins, and Jai wastes no time in digging in. He dips a fry in ketchup and chews.

The moment is lost. And I forget about whatever I wanted to ask as my hunger takes control. I can't be expected to pay attention when there's a plate of fresh, hot fries waiting for me.

I really don't look up until I've taken my last bite, which is when I notice Jai staring at me.

"What?" I ask.

"Here." Jai hands me a napkin. "You have ketchup on your face." I take it and wipe my mouth.

Jai shakes his head. "You missed a spot." He laughs and leans forward to dab at the ketchup, slowly. Our eyes meet.

I don't move.

I don't breathe.

I can't even think.

Our eyes never leave each other.

"All done," he says with a satisfied grin.

I'm pretty sure my heart does that cliché thing of skipping a beat. I take a sip of my drink, find ice, and start chewing it. It is suddenly very hot in this diner—*too* hot.

Jai asks for the bill while I do everything in my power not to look at him. We go dutch.

"We should head back," Jai says.

And so we head back to Wychwood High, and for the rest of the day I relive that moment at Big Mo's over and over.

It's after school, and I'm sitting in Jai's car again. Jai, Liam, and I are currently on our way to what will be the first official rehearsal with me as lead singer of Infinite Sorrow. I feel oddly calm about everything. Okay, that's a lie. My heart is racing, and my palms are slightly sweaty, and I haven't even stood before the microphone yet. But I want to do this. To beat Ross

Sherman. For my twelve-year-old scared-camper self. For me now.

For Jai.

I *can* do it. And I will.

Jai pulls up to his two-story house, which looks like every other building on the street. It's in the nicer part of town. Jai's mom is an event planner, and her fundraising gala for Wychwood Memorial is the highlight of every year. It's how she knows Mom. It seems all the boys I like have parents who are somehow connected to the hospital. My ex-boyfriend's dad is on the board.

Just as Jai parks in the driveway behind a pearl-white sedan, someone climbs out of it.

"Hey, Farrah," Liam says as she walks toward the house. Jai has two sisters—an older one, Farrah, and a younger one, Kamala. Liam's crush on Farrah is well known. Already his ears are the same red as his hair.

"Hi, Liam," Farrah says. She looks at me. "Hi, Nate."

I wave. Her resemblance to Jai strikes me. It always does.

"Mom has a massive event, so she'll be late. I'm getting delivery. Is pizza okay with you guys?" Farrah asks.

"Yeah, thanks," Jai says.

"Well, I'll leave you to it, then." Farrah shuts the front door behind her.

I follow Jai down the side of the house to the converted bungalow in the backyard. Ms. Patel has invested in her son's talent and passion. What was once a guest house has been fully renovated and is now Infinite Sorrow's rehearsal space and recording studio.

The band went on hiatus when Jai first moved to Wychwood, and that hiatus soon turned permanent when the rest of the members quit. So Jai had to start over from scratch.

The first member he found was Raquel Sánchez, the bass guitarist. Raquel is Farrah's best friend, and she and Jai just hit it off musically. Though she's a junior in college, like Farrah, she still manages to keep up with the band's schedule.

Jai recruited Simon Wilson, the keyboardist, from a classical music competition. Simon is our age but homeschooled. His parents were all for the idea of him broadening his horizons and making friends. I don't think they ever expected the band to actually get popular.

Ross and Jai became friends through school. And that's how he ended up as the lead singer.

Liam pushes between us, and he throws himself on the leather couch by the large amp on the side of the room. He reaches for his drumsticks and beats an imaginary drum for a few seconds. Liam is a recent addition to the band. The previous drummer left a few months ago, and Liam joined through an audition.

Simon and Raquel show up ten minutes after we arrive.

"I'm sorry, but what is this bullshit?" Raquel asks as she sits on the couch. She has brown skin, black hair, and dark eyes. "Ross betrayed us."

"For the record, I'd like to say that I never liked him," Simon says. He is short, with brown hair and pale skin.

"You don't like anyone, Si," Raquel snipes.

Simon pushes up his round-rimmed glasses. "True."

I fight a smile. I've spent a lot of time with the band before, and I've always enjoyed it.

"Yeah, Ross screwed us over," Jai says. "But Nate has volunteered to replace him for Ready2Rock." He pats my shoulder.

"For the record, I'd like to say that I've always liked Nate," Simon says.

I laugh. "Thanks, Si. I appreciate it." Being with the band is making me feel less nervous.

"So—what? Are we sticking to the same set list as before?" Raquel asks.

Jai nods. "Since Nate knows our songs by heart, I don't think we need to change much."

"Hmm. This wasn't actually a crisis, then," Raquel says. "I thought it was a bullet wound, but all we needed was a Band-Aid." She points at me, and I wave.

Jai laughs. "Well, without Nate it would have been a disaster. So we all owe him one."

"Okay, enough with the flattery," Liam says. "Can we just play something? I have to be home before dinner."

"Right, practice." Jai claps. "Let's start with 'Antihero.'" He gives me a knowing look. It's a song that Jai has heard me sing countless times. I smile. With Jai on my side, I know I can do this.

Everyone takes their positions, and so do I—front and center. Jai holds out a mic, and after a moment's hesitation, I grab it.

"You've got this," Jai assures me. My heart starts to race, but I try to ignore it.

The first chord echoes, and I close my eyes. I don't think of anyone else. It's just me alone. I sing this song in the shower all the time. I know it so well that I can recite all the words with or without music.

I exhale and let go of my fear and nerves.

This is my cue.

I open my eyes and start to sing.

And just like that I, Nathan Hargreaves, become the lead singer of Infinite Sorrow.

6

I'm heading to the cafeteria and going over my lyrics in my head. Halfway there, Gemma links her right arm with mine. I turn to her, startled.

"What are you thinking about so hard?" she asks, and flicks the lines on my forehead.

"Ouch!" I rub the spot she hit.

Gemma is wearing another of her creations today. A hot-pink dress paired with a sleeveless jacket and ankle boots.

"Seriously, what's up?" she asks as we enter the cafeteria.

"I'm just wondering if I can actually pull off singing with Infinite Sorrow," I say. Right after band practice ended last night, I texted Gemma everything that had happened. Of course, she already knew because this is high school and the rumor mill never stops churning.

In the cafeteria, crimson-and-gold banners hang from the walls in support of the Titans. Students bustle around the lunch line and between the red tables that fill the space. Gemma and I join the queue.

"I think you're talented enough to outsing Ross even on

your worst day," Gemma says. "You just need some confidence is all."

I laugh. "I'm not sure about that, but thanks."

Gemma nudges me with an elbow. "That's what best friends are for. We're here to inflate egos and bash the competition. Two things I do very well."

We each take a slice of meat-surprise pizza. Gemma holds up her plate and studies it for a moment. "Do you think they deliberately try to make these meals look as unappealing as possible?"

It's true Wychwood's cafeteria food is, in one word, a disaster.

"I mean, it should be impossible to ruin pizza, and yet here we are," I say. "Everyone involved should be charged for this crime. Immediately."

We sit at our usual table. "Oh, did you hear about our resident 'it' couple?" Gemma asks.

"Brody and Kate?"

She nods. "Apparently there's trouble in paradise."

"Already! It's been, like, what? Less than two weeks?" It is no secret that Brody Miller's relationships do not last, but surely this must be some sort of new record.

"What's been less than two weeks?" Jai asks. He sits down next to Gemma.

I take a tentative bite of the "pizza" while Gemma brings Jai up to speed.

"I didn't realize that Brody was dating Kate," Jai admits. "I thought he was still with Stefanie."

"Keeping up with the romances of Brody Miller is like a

full-time job," Gemma says. Her phone vibrates, and she does a little happy dance when she looks at her screen. "Ah!"

"What is it?" I ask.

"I just got an internship for the summer! It's, like, one hundred percent confirmed that I'll be working for Oscar Gomez, who is this up-and-coming designer who specializes in avant-garde designs. He is a pioneer of haute couture and such a risk-taker. His looks have been worn at the major red carpets."

"I understand only about half of what you just said," I say, "but I'm happy for you. You really wanted this."

Gemma claps. "It will look so good on my college applications."

"And there she goes," Jai teases. To Gemma there is nothing more important than college applications. I'm keeping all my fingers and toes crossed for her to get in. The alternative is too scary to think about. Come on, universe, please don't let me down.

"Try to at least remember to enjoy the experience," I say.

"Everything about fashion is fun," Gemma says. "Of course I'm going to enjoy it. It's LA. Even if it means sleeping on Tori's couch for two weeks, I'm okay with it." Gemma rolls her eyes at the thought of her older sister. I'm pretty sure they have been in a love-hate relationship since Gemma was born.

"So you both will be AWOL this summer." Jai makes an exaggerated pout that has no business being as cute as it is.

"Just for the first two weeks," I say.

"I'm so jealous," Gemma whines. "An all-expenses-paid trip to South Africa. God, I want wealthy family members."

"How rich are they?" Jai asks.

"I think they're one of the richest families not just in South Africa but in, like, all of Africa. Quite possibly among the one percent of the world, to be honest," I say with a shrug.

Jai whistles. "So your cousin's wedding will be one hell of an event?"

I nod. "I'll probably never experience something like it ever again."

After band practice on Friday evening, Jai and I are hanging out in his room. It isn't my first time in Jai's bedroom. He's invited me to stay for dinner, and with Mom working, I happily said yes.

This whole week, Jai and I got together to practice one-on-one. That's on top of band rehearsals. Joining Infinite Sorrow has come with the added benefit of spending way more time with Jai than I used to.

Jai's room is much bigger than mine. Next to a messily made double bed there's a desk covered in sheet music, and one of his guitars stands in the corner of the room. Posters of bands like Queen, Nirvana, Oasis, and Aerosmith cover one wall. Clothes that should be in a hamper carpet the floor. I guess it's true that opposites attract.

We head downstairs to find the women of the Patel house already seated at the table. Even with her busy schedule, Ms. Patel makes sure to have at least one family dinner each week, most times on a Friday.

I slide in between Jai and his younger sister. Kamala, with

her dark brown skin and curly black hair, looks the most like her mom. She's reading *A Game of Magic and Mayhem*, the first book in a popular fantasy series. Kamala may be thirteen, but she's dead set on becoming a writer.

For tonight's menu, Ms. Patel and Farrah prepared butter chicken with a side of naan bread. There's also some yogurt, salad, and achar on the table. The aroma has my mouth watering. It's also cleansing my lungs after the stench of Wychwood High's failed attempt at meat loaf.

"The naan is from the store. I had a caterer flake at work, so I had to stay later than expected," Ms. Patel explains. She joins us at the table, and we begin to eat. "How's band practice going, you guys?"

"Not bad," Jai replies. "Nate really saved us this time."

"I didn't know you could sing, Nate," Ms. Patel says.

"And he's so good at it!" Farrah adds. When we turn to her with questioning looks, she shrugs. "I heard some of the practice."

"I'm trying my best," I say. I don't tell them about my stage fright. So far it's been a secret kept just between Jai and me. Even though I perform well in practice, I'm still a little worried about being onstage. But Jai says he'll help me get over it when I come back from South Africa.

Good luck with that one!

For now, Jai says I should focus on getting comfortable with the songs we'll be performing. So that is what I'm doing.

"Any plans for summer break?" Ms. Patel asks me.

"My cousin's getting married in South Africa," I say. "So, Mom and I are flying out there for two weeks."

"That sounds wonderful," Ms. Patel says. "I didn't know you had family there."

"That beats my plans. I'll also be away . . . at college. Having summer classes." Farrah groans. "You know, the glamorous life of a college student."

"Which means I'll be able to focus on editing my novel," Kamala says. Turning to her sister, she chides, "Farrah always has friends over."

Farrah sticks out her tongue. The two sisters begin teasing each other.

"Just ignore them," Jai advises. "I do most of the time." He reaches for a second helping of food, and I follow his lead. Having such a lively dinner is strange. At home, it's always been just Mom and me. But eating with a bigger family like this is nice.

Especially because it's Jai's family.

7

It's Sunday night and I am home alone. With Mom being a nurse, I'm used to this. When I was growing up, it was rough when she needed to work late. But now that I'm a junior, this feels normal.

I check my phone. I mean, a prepacking break can't hurt. I've put this off for weeks, so what's another twenty minutes? I end up on Instagram, and I'm scrolling when I see a post from my cousin Meghan. She's looking all bridal in a white cocktail dress. I read the caption.

> Last time seeing my friends stateside
> before the wedding. See you all in sunny
> S.A. #PreWeddingBash #21DaystoGo
> #HereComestheBride

I swipe right and look through other pictures in the gallery. In the last photo, my cousin's standing in the middle of a crowd of friends, all raising a glass to her. There's a girl who's definitely had too much to drink, a guy who's so excited you'd think he was the bride, and then—

Tommy?!

It's him. I mean, *him*.

Tommy Herron. *My* Tommy. I mean, not *my* Tommy, not anymore.

My ex-boyfriend.

But still, it's Tommy. Somehow, Thomas James Herron is there, standing in a picture with my cousin.

I am not okay.

Seriously, what the actual hell is going on?

I tap the picture and find that the girl standing next to Tommy has an Instagram account: @Erikaonthecoast. Before I know it, I'm on her page, several posts deep. Then one photo knocks the air out of my lungs.

It's a picture of her and Tommy—kissing, with the beach in the distance.

I continue scrolling and stop at another picture. This one is of Tommy smiling directly into the camera. He looks happy and healthy. His brown hair is longer than I've seen it.

My eyes snag on the caption and a wave of nausea hits me.

With my love.

I stare at my phone, unblinking. Tommy ghosted me, and this is the first thing I've seen of him since last summer.

I keep scrolling until the photos of Tommy stop—which takes a while. There is a picture of Erika and Tommy sitting around a campfire. It was a trip with her family. There's one of them at the movies, which feels like a punch to the gut because my first date with Tommy was to see a superhero movie. At the time we didn't call it a date. I think we were both too scared to admit to whatever we were. In the dark of the theater, surrounded by shadows and the flickering silver light, Tommy mustered up the courage to take my hand in his. It was a small moment, but it changed everything.

That was the start of us, and this right here feels like the final piece to our ending. It's clear that Tommy and this girl—Erika—have been friends for years. I'm not sure what that means for me and my relationship with him, because ours never officially ended. I'm confused, and hurt, and above all else angry.

Sometimes you think your wounds have healed. And then life throws you a fistful of salt and you squirm in pain.

I send a quick text to Meghan.

> Hey, I just saw your post on Insta. You know Tommy Herron?

She replies a few minutes later:

> He's my best friend's boyfriend. He's her plus-one for the wedding. You know him?

> Yeah. We went to the same school.

If only it were that simple between Tommy and me. We were so much more.

Meghan and I chat for a few more minutes, but I'm not feeling it, so I find a way to quickly end the convo. I bury my face in my hands and scream, thankful that I am home alone. I don't care about getting a noise complaint from Mr. Schuster.

Well, shit! This is not how I wanted to feel about this trip.

The thought of seeing him with his new girlfriend is like a knife to the heart.

I dive into bed, put on my headphones, and start blasting music. A song by Billie Eilish comes on. I don't want to think. So I let song after song take my mind away from things.

———

Hours later, I'm still thinking about Tommy. I've fallen down a rabbit hole and opened those forbidden texts of ours. My eyes are misty as I study a photo of us at his junior-senior prom. I went with Gemma. Well, technically I went alone, as the third wheel to Gemma and this junior guy who was her date.

Of course, I spent the evening making eyes at my boyfriend—a secret from everyone except Gemma. Tommy Herron looked fantastic that night. He was wearing a black-and-white tuxedo, and his dark hair was pushed back.

Occasionally, we would sneak off. We even spent a few minutes making out under the bleachers. That night, it felt like everything was possible for our relationship. We had a future. I was the happiest I'd ever been, and I thought we would last.

And we did, for a few more months at least, until Tommy graduated and I was left behind.

My eyes snag on the box that I've kept hidden on my closet floor. I brought it home from Big Mo's. It once stored napkins but now keeps the physical reminders of my first relationship.

I haven't opened it in months, fearing that I'd unravel feelings I've successfully kept in check. I loved Tommy Herron with all my heart. And I'll probably always remember him because he was my first: first boy I told I was gay, first kiss, first time, and first love.

But along with the good I'll always remember the bad too. Like how he broke my heart into a million little pieces for no apparent reason.

I kneel and pull the box toward me. It's slightly dusty. I open it and find all the mementos that remind me I dated Tommy.

Right on top is the sweater that Tommy lent me on our first date. It was extremely windy, and I'd gotten cold. I knew I'd fallen for Tommy when he offered me his sweater. I meant to give it back to him, but at the time I loved having this keepsake—the smell of him, his sandalwood cologne.

I pick up a strip of photos we took in a photo booth at Indigo Pier, the amusement park in Fairvale. Tommy and I drove there on a Saturday, and it was one of the best days of my life. We walked hand in hand. Proud to be together, to be gay, to be happy.

I make a move to look through more of my relationship with Tommy, but I stop myself. I don't need to do this. I lived it all. I felt it all. Reliving these moments will only hurt me.

With a sigh, I close and pick up the box. I'm finally ready to do it.

I leave the apartment and head down to the garbage cans in front of our building.

After I've thrown it out, I feel better. I pull out my phone and finally delete all our old text messages. Yes, there are tears in my eyes, and yes, my heart hurts, and yes, I stand there longer than I should.

With a sigh, I put my phone away.

This is letting go.

I spent most of the night tossing and turning and thinking of all the possible scenarios in which I could encounter my ex-boyfriend on this trip.

I exit my bedroom in the morning and find Mom sitting at the kitchen table. I went to bed without seeing her last night. Mom is drinking a freshly brewed cup of coffee, and she's dressed for work. "Morning," I say. And then I notice the look on her face. "What's wrong?"

"My leave has been canceled," Mom says.

"Why?" I ask.

"I have to cover for Nina," Mom explains. "She had a heart attack."

"Oh no. Is she okay?"

Mom nods. "She's in recovery now. The surgery went well." Mom puts her coffee cup down. "I'm sorry, Sonno."

And with that, Mom delivers the final nail in the coffin of this trip.

"What are you saying?" I ask. "You don't mean you're missing the wedding, right?" I can't hide the disappointment in my voice. I need Mom to come. Even though she knows nothing about Tommy and me, her being there would help.

"Unfortunately, yes. My hands are tied. I couldn't really

fight them on this." Mom sighs. "The higher-ups hold all the power."

The mention of "higher-ups" makes me think of my ex-boyfriend's father, but I don't share that information with Mom. As far as she is concerned, I have never dated.

I didn't mean to keep it from her, but Tommy and I started dating before I came out to Mom, so it was a confusing time. Neither of us felt comfortable sharing our relationship, or even talking about our sexuality, with our parents just yet. Now that we're broken up, I don't think I ever need to tell Mom about Tommy—or want to, if I'm being honest.

"Well, this sucks," I say. I don't add "donkey balls" because I am in the presence of Mom. But I think it. *This well and truly sucks donkey balls.*

"I'm sorry, Sonno," Mom says. "I know how excited you were about the trip. I hope you still go. Everything's already been fully paid for. I think it would be a shame if both of us miss out. But of course, the decision is yours."

Mom has always been my shield, and without her, this trip could be a bloody battle.

Still, a million thoughts are running through my head. *We already have the tickets. It's too late to cancel. And I don't want to. I still want to go. But Mom . . .*

"I'm really sorry, Nate," Mom says again.

I shake my head. "Don't be—it's not your fault."

But as I pour myself a cup of coffee, my mood darkens. The headache that's been threatening to hit all morning finally does. And it only intensifies as we drive to school. I'm silent and sullen, with way too much on my mind.

I become increasingly frustrated with the sudden change in plans. I arrive at school and close the car door with a loud bang. I know it isn't Mom's fault, but I can't help it. I keep my head down and my brow furrowed through my first three classes. We're halfway through third period when Jai nudges me.

"What's wrong?" he asks. His voice is low, and it's clear from his expression that he's really concerned.

I sigh. "Last night I found out Tommy will be at my cousin's wedding."

"What!" Jai says loudly. Several people turn to look at him, but he seems unbothered by their glances. "How is that possible?" Jai never met Tommy in person, but he knows all about the epic failure of our relationship.

"Apparently he is dating my cousin's best friend, Erika," I respond.

"Holy shit!" Jai says. "So you'll have to see him after he ghosted you? That's bullshit!"

I nod. "And here's the kicker," I say. "I'll be dealing with this all alone."

"What do you mean?" Jai asks.

"My mom can't make it to the wedding after all. I'm thinking of going solo," I say.

"Are you sure?" Jai asks.

The truth is, I'm torn. "Not to get too serious or emotional, but going to the wedding is important to me. I don't want to let Tommy ruin that. I don't know. I was kind of excited to see where my dad lived when he was my age." I shrug. "It may seem silly, but this feels like a chance I'll never get again."

Jai nods. "Then you definitely should go," he says. "And it's not silly. I totally get why this trip is important to you."

"But Tommy," I grumble. "That asshole is still messing up my life."

"Hmmm," Jai says. He seems to be deep in thought.

The bell rings and we grab our bags.

"You know, you could ask one of us to go with you," Jai says as we make it out into the hallway. I don't realize he's stopped moving until I walk into him.

"Huh?" I ask.

Jai looks me dead in the eye. We're standing pretty close to one another.

"I know Gemma has that internship with the big fancy designer in LA this summer, so she won't be able to go. But I could."

It takes me a moment to realize what Jai's offering.

Wait, what?

"You'd come with me to South Africa?" I ask.

"If the ticket's transferable, sure," Jai laughs.

"Really?" I can't help but be surprised.

"It's a free trip," Jai says. "But more than that, if it's to support you, of course I'd come."

As a friend? I want to ask. But I'm not brave enough. Even if this isn't a romantic gesture, my heart is hammering a hole through my chest.

"You'd have to ask your mom," I point out.

"You know she'll be okay with it," Jai says. "She loves you."

"What about band stuff?" I ask.

"Well, you're our lead singer now, so we couldn't really practice much without you. Besides, you know all our songs, so we'll be fine," Jai says.

"But what about—" I start, but Jai cuts me off.

"Are you done making excuses?" He raises an eyebrow and rests a hand on my shoulder. "Come on, Nate. I'll be your plus-one."

And the way he's looking at me, I can't say no. I don't want to say no.

So I nod. "Yes."

Jai smiles and turns to leave, but I can't move. My knees are jelly.

Oh God, what if he finds out how I feel? What does that mean for our friendship?

If Jai comes with me, it'll be two weeks with the boy I like—alone.

8

It's my last day of junior year, and Mom just got another speeding ticket. But not even that dampens my mood, because after the final bell today, we will be free at last.

Tomorrow Jai and I will be off to South Africa.

I'm still a little surprised that Ms. Patel agreed to let Jai come with me, but I'm so glad that she did. Jai said it was easier to convince his mom to let him come on this trip than to get her to allow him to compete in Ready2Rock. I have to admit I'm barely thinking about Tommy now that I know Jai and I will be together in South Africa.

"Thanks for the ride, Farrah," I say.

"No worries," she says.

Jai and I are in his sister's car on the way to my apartment. We have an early flight tomorrow, so Jai is sleeping over. Truth be told, I've never had a boy sleep over—let alone one I like.

Tommy came over from time to time when we were dating, but that was always during the day, and he always left just before Mom got home.

"What are you thinking about?" Jai asks. He chose to sit next to me in the back seat just to annoy his sister.

I snap out of it. "What?"

"You were smiling," Jai says. "I was wondering what you were thinking about."

You.

I want to answer, but I'm not brave enough to say it. More and more I want to tell Jai how I feel. Jai is bi. Being a guy isn't the thing that's holding me back. In part, it's that I worry he'll reject me and it will ruin everything between us.

But I think the larger part of it is that I've been burned by love before, and those scars are still healing.

We pull into the parking lot of my apartment building, and Farrah parks the car.

"You two have a great time," Farrah says. "And take photos!"

"I will," I say.

"You have a great time too," Jai adds.

Farrah glares at him, knowing full well that he's referring to her summer classes. Jai smiles and waves.

I help him carry his bags into the apartment. As my friend, Jai's obviously been to my place before, but never at night, and somehow the time of day changes everything.

We enter, and I immediately regret that I waited for Mom in the car this morning, when I should've used the time to clean up. The living room is a disaster, but I know my room is clean. I'm thankful for my neat-by-nature trait, which I'm told is another thing I inherited from my dad. Maybe if he were still around, I'd be able to convince Mom that her dirty clothes do not belong on our sofa but in the laundry.

Unfortunately, it is a battle that I am losing.

"Sorry about the mess," I say.

"No worries," Jai says. "You know my room is ten times worse than this."

I lead him through the living room to my bedroom, and on the way I pick up some of Mom's clothes.

Jai walks over to my keyboard and twiddles a few keys. He stops when his eyes snag on my empty fishbowl. He raises an eyebrow in question.

"Beyoncé died," I say. "So now I'm just a weirdo who keeps an empty bowl of water in his bedroom."

Jai laughs. "We should go get a replacement when we get back."

"Deal," I say. It always thrills me to make plans with Jai, even the mundane ones. I'm cool with mundane. Unlike love, mundane never hurt anybody.

"So do you want something to drink? Water or . . ." I trail off because I remember the state of our fridge. With Mom's busy schedule, grocery shopping is usually done on weekends, so we have nothing on hand. We're not ready for guests. "Actually, I think we just have water," I finish.

Jai laughs. "No worries, water's fine."

"Be right back," I say. I make a beeline for Mom's bathroom to throw her clothes into the hamper before heading to the kitchen for a glass of water. When I return to my room, Jai's still playing my keyboard. And he looks so good.

Ogling and holding drinks should not be mixed. As I'm walking over to Jai, I trip. It all happens in slow motion. Jai stands to get out of the way, but by then it's already too late. I've splashed him with the glass of water, and the front of his shirt is completely drenched.

"Shit!" I exclaim, and look at him, horrified. "I'm so sorry."

"It's okay, Nate." He smiles and then laughs. I grab a towel from my cupboard and rush to wipe him down. My hand travels across his chest. And I freeze.

Jai is as still as me. I look up, and our eyes meet. We're so close to each other.

"Uh, I'll give you a fresh shirt." I head to my closet and get a clean T-shirt. Jai pulls his shirt off. I guess I suggested this outfit change, so I should've known what the outcome would be . . . Jai Patel shirtless in my bedroom.

Dear God, I was not ready for this.

I swear I stop breathing. All of a sudden, I remember that Jai used to be a competitive swimmer. With his broad shoulders, it shows.

If I could draw anything besides stick figures, I would want to draw Jai Patel—at this moment, as the afternoon sun streams in through my bedroom window, the light casting shadows on his taut skin.

Jai Patel is beautiful. There is no other way to describe him. His profile reminds me of those Greek statues I've seen in books. I think I finally understand what people mean when they say they have muses.

I scold myself for thinking about my friend like this, when

he is shirtless and we are alone in my bedroom. I look away, a little too late. He's caught me staring.

I need to snap out of it.

"Uh, sorry," I say. I can't fight the flush from my face. I hold out the fresh shirt, and he takes it.

"No problem." Jai smiles. As he unfolds the shirt, I catch sight of his tattoo. The wing design covers the scar that runs from his collarbone to his shoulder. I knew about Jai's injury, but this is actually the first time I've seen the scar. Jai was in a car accident a few years ago. A drunk driver ran a red light. He has pins in his shoulder now, but luckily he's alive.

Jai catches me staring . . . *again.*

I hear the front door opening and use that chance to exit stage left. I don't exactly run out of my bedroom, but I do something just shy of it.

"Mom, what are you doing here?" I ask.

"I live here," Mom says, as if that's what I'm asking. She has her arms full of groceries.

"No, I mean you're home early."

"Yeah, I want to make dinner for you and Jai." Mom is an excellent cook. She doesn't have the time to cook very often, but when she does, the food is amazing.

I'm helping Mom put the groceries away when Jai comes out of my room.

Jai is slightly taller than me; he's also way more muscular, so my shirt hugs his body tightly. I try my best to ignore this but fail. *Damn it, teen hormones.*

"Hey, Ms. Hargreaves," Jai says.

"Hi, Jai." Mom shows him her best smile. I'm pretty sure Mom liked Jai even before I did. I've never shared my crush on Jai with her, but something in the looks she shoots me when Jai is around tells me that she already knows.

Sometimes it's a real bother how well Mom knows me. Still, I plan on telling her about my next relationship. I don't ever want to date anyone in secret again.

The hardest thing wasn't keeping the relationship from her, but rather not telling her about the breakup. I needed her by my side, assuring me that it would all be okay and that it wasn't my fault.

9

D-day.

I am not a morning person—I have never been and probably will never be—so the fact that I am up before the sun and currently heading to the airport is a crime against humanity. And the universe will be hearing from my lawyers.

Though San Diego is the closer city, we're on our way to LAX, which means a two-hour car ride. Or, as I like to think of it, two hours for me to catch up on lost sleep.

"Should I turn the radio on?" Mom asks.

"Mom, are you trying to punish me?" I turn to her. "Do you hate me?"

"Stop being so dramatic, Nate," Mom says. She glances in the rearview mirror and catches sight of Jai in the back seat. "Look at Jai—he's all bright-eyed."

I groan and turn to study him, my eyelids weighing heavy. Mom's right. The sun is just now starting to rise, but Jai appears fresh. Which isn't that surprising, to be honest. I'm sure he'd look fresh after a week of sleep deprivation.

Jai's wearing track pants and a black hoodie, and he has his headphones on. His hair is tied into a messy top bun. I used to say I hated man buns, but looking at Jai Patel, I've been converted.

Jai smiles and I give him the side-eye. It's unfair that he's capable of showing happiness right now.

"I told you to have an early night," Mom says. As if that were so easy, considering that Jai slept mere feet away from me. I tossed and I turned and I fantasized—sue me, I'm a teenage boy.

"I tried. But my brain would not let me, and so here I am. Four hours later." I close my eyes. "Can we please just be quiet?"

"This is the last time that I'm going to see you for two weeks. That's the longest we have been separated. Allow me to enjoy this."

I groan. "We should've just taken Jai's car."

"Moms before friends," Mom says. Then she leans in closer and whispers into my ear, "Moms before boyfriends too."

"Mom, what are you talking about? Stop," I plead.

Mom laughs. "Any boy who is willing to be your plus-one to a family wedding is a keeper." We stop at a red light and she turns to me again. "On that note, I want you to be safe."

It takes a moment for me to register what Mom is talking about. My eyes shoot open. Well, I'm fully awake now.

I turn to look at Jai, but his eyes are closed. Thank God he's wearing his headphones. "Mom, you are not going to give me the birds-and-bees talk before the sun has even fully risen," I whisper. "And you are definitely not going to do it with Jai in the back seat."

God, this is so embarrassing.

"If not now, when?" Mom asks, completely unbothered. She takes off when the light turns green.

"I am not going to . . . ya know." I keep my eyes trained on the glove compartment. I do not want to be having this conversation with Mom right now. How much worse would this all be if she knew for certain about my massive crush on Jai?

"You never know what can happen. Either way, I want you to be safe," Mom continues. I reach for the door handle. I remember that scene in *Lady Bird* where Saoirse Ronan jumps out of a moving car. I'm tempted to do the same. But I'm not trying to injure myself. Regardless, I appreciate Lady Bird's spirit, and so I channel it now.

"I'm leaving," I say. "I am willing to walk to the airport."

Mom sighs. "Why are you so dramatic?"

"Geez, Mom, it must be because of who raised me?" I smile. "Plus one of my best friends lives and breathes fashion, and the other is in a rock band. How can I not be dramatic?"

"Smart-ass," Mom says.

I reach for the radio. Anything to stop Mom from killing me with her embarrassing questions.

Eventually I doze off. Maybe it's because I'm going to South Africa that I dream of Dad. Or at least a version of him that my mind has stitched together from memories—not my own, but from the stories Mom's told me of him.

In the dream, Dad and I are sitting on the couch playing a video game. It's something I'll never get to do in real life. It is one of the million things—big and small—that I will never get to experience with him.

I'm in the midst of a different dream when Mom nudges me awake. I blink against the sunlight. We've arrived. I stretch as Mom parks. Sleeping in the car is never comfortable, so my body aches, but desperate times call for desperate measures.

I'm not really a big fan of crowded places, so I hate airports. It's still early morning, but all around me people are buzzing. After we get our boarding passes, we carefully maneuver our way to the TSA.

When we get there, Mom pulls me close. "I'll see you in two weeks, Sonno."

"I'll be fine, Mom," I say.

"I know. You're brave and strong and perfect. Remember that." I nuzzle into her curls. There is no other smell in this world as comforting as your mom's.

"Take care, Jai," Mom says.

"I will. Be safe on your trip home," Jai says.

Jai and Mom share a smile before we turn to get in line. I look over my shoulder and see Mom waving as we're eaten by the crowd.

"You ready?" he asks me. I know that he's asking if I'm ready for more than just the flight.

I shrug, and it's the best answer I can give. The truth is, I don't really know if I'm ready. I have so many unresolved feelings as far as Tommy is concerned. Add to that my feelings for Jai, and I am just one giant mess of emotions.

Jai must pick up on my distress, because he takes me by the hand and leads me on.

He doesn't let go either. And I don't complain.

Maybe this trip will be the perfect opportunity for me to finally come clean with Jai. I cannot help but fantasize about this being the most epic first date in the history of first dates . . . but no. I stop myself. That's not what this is.

I won't trick myself into thinking that.

10

Twenty-five hours and one layover later, we touch down at O. R. Tambo International Airport. My legs feel stiff as we squeeze out of the airplane. I pause and take a deep breath of fresh air before we step down onto the runway for the first time. This is South Africa. I am actually here in Johannesburg— Jozi, the City of Gold.

It's midday, and the sun is bright overhead. Jai turns to me with a beaming smile. We follow the crowd to our luggage.

"Nathan!" Aunt Sylvia screams. We cross a gate to reach her. She is tall and lithe, with brown skin, dark brown hair, and green eyes. Aunt Sylvia is glamorous. There's no other word to describe her. She's wearing a white suit that's probably some designer brand I can't pronounce. Her shoes are red-bottomed, and her ears are gold-studded. Mom often jokes that when she and Aunt Sylvia are talking about carrots, they mean two very different things. Though I guess both the vegetable and the gold are covered in dust at some point.

Aunt Sylvia married my dad's older and only brother, Richard, much to her family's chagrin. They felt he wasn't good enough, being a mechanic and the son of small-scale farmers. Richard and Sylvia's marriage was especially scandalous because she was an heir to a mining conglomerate. From what Mom has told me, Sylvia doesn't really speak to her family much anymore. She sold her shares in the mine and opened her first hotel. Several hotels later—hotels all around the world—she's made of money. Aunt Sylvia chose love and was better for it in the end.

"Hey, Aunt Sylvia." She pulls me into a hug and squeezes me. I've always loved Aunt Sylvia—she's fun. She also happens to be my godmother.

She holds me at arm's length and looks me up and down. "You've grown since the last time I saw you. What has it been, a year already?"

I nod. Aunt Sylvia and Meghan visited when Meghan went back to Stanford for her final year. "Yeah, almost."

"I'm really upset your mom can't make it." Aunt Sylvia pouts. "I even considered buying the hospital just to get her here." I know she's joking, but the truth is that she *could* actually buy the hospital if she wanted to, which makes her statement almost believable.

Aunt Sylvia turns to Jai. "And this is . . . ?"

He introduces himself. "I'm Jai."

"Oh yes," Aunt Sylvia says. "Your mom mentioned you were coming with a friend." She looks between Jai and me. "Just a friend?"

"Aunt Sylvia! Yes, friends." Jai and I both turn to look at each other. I want nothing more than to be Jai's boyfriend. Jai laughs.

"Okay, I won't pry," Aunt Sylvia says with a soft chuckle of her own. "Let's go."

We load our luggage into the back of Aunt Sylvia's sleek black Mercedes SUV. Jai is extra careful as he sets his precious guitar down. I don't know much about cars—to me they are just lumps of metal with four wheels—but even I'm impressed. And I know this is only the start. Aunt Sylvia and Co. are rich AF.

Jai leans over to me. "I know you told me your family was rich, but seeing is believing."

I nod. A few months back Aunt Sylvia was even in a *Forbes* roundup titled "Ten African Businesswomen Paving the Way."

"Are you sure you want to stay with Ouma Lettie?" Aunt Sylvia asks as she climbs into the car. We follow suit, me in the front and Jai in the back. Aunt Sylvia starts the car with the push of a button. While it idles, she fishes a pair of Gucci shades from the glove compartment. "The rest of the wedding guests have rooms at one of our hotels. We could get one for you too. It's no problem at all."

"The rest of the wedding guests" includes Tommy, and I most certainly do not want to stay near him.

Even before I knew that Tommy was coming to the wedding, I said no to staying at the hotel with the other guests. *Good job, past Nate!* I want to spend time with Ouma Lettie. She feels like the only link I have to Dad and who he was when he was my age.

Mom doesn't have those memories. She met him later. This is the best chance I'm ever going to get to know my dad.

I shrug. "I think it'll be nice to spend time with Ouma Lettie. I don't really get to see her that much."

"Understood," Aunt Sylvia says. "I'm sure she's going to love having you there. Both of you. She's always looking for extra hands around the farm. I keep telling her to sell it, but she insists that she'll die there. I understand, though. It's been in her family for years." Aunt Sylvia looks over to me. "By the way, Ouma Lettie has a copy of the itinerary for the two weeks. We have a lot planned. If any of the events interest you, I'll happily send a driver over to get you. Just let me know. I'm sure that Meghan would love to spend as much time with you as possible, but being the bride means she's super busy." Aunt Sylvia hits the gas. "Don't take it personally."

"I won't," I say. "This is all about her. I'm happy for her." Meghan is my only first cousin. Sad to say, Mom is an only child too. I once asked her why she chose to only have me. Apparently, she'd experienced enough baby poop and tears to last a lifetime. I was her precious, perfect bundle of joy, and that was plenty. I really couldn't argue with that.

"We're hosting a banquet for all the guests a few days before the wedding—we expect that you'll join us. Everything else is optional, save for the actual wedding. We have so much planned. Your uncle Richard wants to host a braai for you sometime while you're here. He makes a mean potjie, so you have to taste it. We also have a wonderful tour of some historic places, including a trip to the Apartheid Museum."

The latter sounds like something I'd enjoy. In history Mr. Ellis taught us briefly about apartheid, but we barely covered anything. That racist bullshit lasted for the better part of fifty years. My dad grew up during apartheid. He was fifteen years old when democracy was introduced in 1994.

"Also, this coming weekend we'll be heading down to the

beach in Durban. We'll fly, of course," Aunt Sylvia continues. "It was a toss-up between there and Cape Town, but who could resist the warm waters of the east coast? It is winter, after all."

Planning a beach trip in winter is so strange to me, and yet it makes sense. I'm pretty sure Africa is the hottest continent in the world. But Aunt Sylvia says the weather is changing. Though it gets chilly during winter, there are still very warm days. *Thanks, global warming!*

It's not just the weather and seasons that are different from what I know in the US. I've been looking up South African English, and lots of words are different too. Trash cans are bins, living rooms are lounges, and gas is petrol.

The most glaring difference at the moment, though, is that we're driving on the left side of the road.

"But I hope you partake," Aunt Sylvia says. "You too, Jai. Please don't let Nate stop you from enjoying this trip. I know my nephew can be something of a wet blanket."

"Sure thing, ma'am," Jai says from the back seat. He's been quiet, looking at the rows of cypresses outside the window. I can't blame him. It's so different from back home.

"I'm not that bad," I tell my aunt.

"Please, your mom says you've never caused any trouble for her. She worries you're not getting the full teenage experience."

"Trust Mom to complain that I am actually a well-behaved teenager."

"She's just worried that you've been forced to grow up too soon," Aunt Sylvia says. "If I'm being honest, I'm worried about that too."

I can't make a fuss about my high school experience. Sure,

it hasn't been the stuff you see in movies or read about in books, but then again, whose life is really like that anyway? High school is what it is—we make the most of it, and then we leave. Being closeted for a while sucked, and coming out brought scrapes and bruises. But I can't really whine about it, because I know that for some people, being out in high school is a real hell. I'm one of the lucky ones. And it sucks that I have to think of myself as fortunate because the world still hates on queer teenagers.

"How far is Ouma Lettie's farm?" I ask.

"About thirty minutes outside the city," Aunt Sylvia says. "Why? Are you tired?"

"Yeah, exhausted." Which is an understatement. I'm way beyond exhausted. My eyes are stinging messes, and I want nothing more than a warm bed to lie down on.

"The trip can be rough," Aunt Sylvia says. "Which is why I tried to convince your mom to at least allow me to upgrade your seats. Of course, she refused."

Mom's like that. She hates wasting money on unnecessary things—especially if it isn't hers in the first place. I'm like that too. Which is why I like working at the diner. I guess it's true when they say that the apple really doesn't fall far from the tree.

I turn around to check on Jai and find that he's dozed off. I smile as Jai's nose twitches in his sleep.

Aunt Sylvia stops the car and says, "These robots are not working, as usual."

"Robots?" I ask. I look around, expecting to see something out of a *Transformers* movie but finding nothing of the sort.

"Oh, traffic lights. It's what we call them here," Aunt Sylvia explains, and I make a mental note to add this to the list of South African terms I should know.

As we drive, the scenery changes. We leave behind the hustle and bustle of the city. Soon vast fields of corn surround us. I'm not used to this much open space. I pop my head out my window and let the breeze meet my face.

In the distance a bird makes a loud noise. It's a strange sound I've never heard before.

"Hadedahs," Aunt Sylvia says. "One of the most annoying things you'll ever hear. They're so loud, they wake up the whole town in the morning."

Another hadedah sounds off, then another. I can see how the noise would get old.

"We've been having lovely weather," Aunt Sylvia muses. "I only hope it holds until the wedding. Winter is the dry season here, but when it rains, it *really* rains."

The car shakes, courtesy of the bumpy road below us, and it pulls me from my thoughts.

"Sorry about that," Aunt Sylvia says. She clicks her tongue. "This road is terrible."

I look around. "Are we there yet?" I ask while fighting a yawn.

"Almost." We make a right turn and approach a gate up a hill. I blink away my sleepiness and look ahead at Ouma Lettie's farm. Aunt Sylvia makes a call, and a moment later the gate opens.

We go in, and I get my first look at where my dad grew up.

11

We drive up toward the farmhouse and park under a large, barren tree. I check my watch out of habit. It's startling to realize that I'm nine hours ahead of back home. It feels like time traveling, and yet we only took an airplane.

The house has two stories, a wraparound porch, and shutters on the windows. The roof is tin, painted red, and the walls are off white. The place is old but well maintained. And it's too big for just one person, but in the past it was home to a family of four. Now only Ouma Lettie lives here, her family divided in half by loss.

Behind the house are a barn and a few animal pens. The sunlight glints off the roofs of the various sheds, and all around are fields of corn and sugarcane.

As we get out of the car, two very large dogs race *directly* toward me. When I say large, I mean mammoth. I have a moment of pure panic, but all these balls of fur do is sniff and lick me. I'm not a fan of dogs—especially big ones—so it's only when they move on to Jai that I let out the breath I've been holding.

Jai seems totally at ease with them. He scratches their

heads, which gets their tails wagging out of control. He bends down and looks under one dog's belly.

"Who's a good girl?" he asks as he rubs her head. When the second dog tackles its way under his palm, Jai does the same thing. "Who's a good boy?"

For as long as I've known Jai, he's always jumped at the chance to pet dogs. He's so cute when he gets excited. It's these small and inconsequential things that have been pulling at my heartstrings throughout our friendship. Jai looks up and our eyes meet.

"How is it that all dogs like you?" I ask.

Jai laughs. "What can I say? I'm completely lovable." Well, he isn't wrong.

I shake my head. "Maybe you should trade in your leather jacket for a white coat."

"Maybe in another life I would," Jai says. "For now, the band is where I want to be."

"Roscoe! Coco!" Aunt Sylvia says with a whistle. "Behave!"

The dogs do a fine job of ignoring her, perfectly content playing with Jai.

Aunt Sylvia sighs. "They only ever listen to Ouma Lettie."

Just then the front door swings open, and I see Ouma Lettie in the flesh for the first time in five years.

On her last visit, Ouma Lettie stayed with us for a week in California. But given her age and health, international travel has become a risk, so we've mostly stuck to Skype.

Ouma Lettie walks to the end of the porch, leaning on a cane she didn't need last time I saw her. Her white skin looks tanned from working in the sun. Ouma Lettie has had black hair the length of her back all her life. Now, at seventy years old, it's all turned gray. It sits in a neat bun on top of her head.

Ouma Lettie looks at me and gives me a smile. It's the subtle sort that doesn't show teeth but still somehow manages to radiate happiness.

Mom says Dad had the same smile. That I have the same smile.

Roscoe and Coco leave Jai behind. The dogs bound up the stairs to stand by Ouma Lettie on the porch. She scratches them behind the ears before turning her attention to us.

"Ouma! I've missed you so much," I say.

"I've missed you too," Ouma Lettie says, wrapping her arms around me. Though I haven't seen her in years, Ouma Lettie has always been a part of my life, so when she hugs me, it isn't awkward or uncomfortable. It feels just right. Maybe some part of me can feel she's my father's mother somehow.

"Uh, Ouma, this is Jai, one of my best friends," I say as we pull apart. "Jai, this is my grandmother."

"It's nice to meet you, ma'am," Jai says.

"You too." Ouma Lettie smiles. "Well, don't just stand there—come on in." She turns on her heel and heads back inside. Jai and I get our luggage from the car.

We close the door and follow Aunt Sylvia into the house. Stepping into the farmhouse feels like stepping back in time. Well, *mostly*—Ouma Lettie has a flat-screen TV to watch all her favorite soaps. The furniture is all old and comfortable. The type of stuff that people would call antique or vintage but that to me is just homey.

The living room—er, the lounge—has two large sofas and a well-used coffee table piled with books and newspapers. The walls are white, and there's a floor-to-ceiling bookshelf opposite the television.

We leave our luggage at the foot of the staircase and trail behind Aunt Sylvia to the kitchen. There Ouma Lettie is busy at the stove. The kitchen is farmhouse style, with all dark wood. The appliances are modern, though. Which is a relief. I'm not a snob by any means, but I'd be lying if I said I wasn't a bit concerned about having to live without certain comforts. I am a twenty-first-century teenager. Sue me.

A home-cooked feast covers the kitchen table from end to end: bacon, sausage, toast, and even some roasted tomatoes.

"You boys traveled a long time." Ouma Lettie turns to Jai and me. "Now come on, wash your hands and eat." She looks at Aunt Sylvia. "Have you eaten? You're nothing but skin and bones."

"Thank you, Ouma," Aunt Sylvia says. "My personal trainer will be happy to hear that. Nothing for me, though. I just came to drop the boys off like I promised Rebecca. She's very worried about Nate, you know."

"I'm not a baby," I grumble as I wash my hands and take a seat at the table.

"No matter how old you get, you'll always be your mother's baby," Ouma Lettie says as she puts a plate of eggs down on the table. "I'll walk you out, Sylvia. You boys eat up."

"Thank you," Jai says.

"Yeah, thanks, Ouma."

Ouma Lettie puts a hand on my shoulder and gently

squeezes it. Like Mom, she still wears her wedding ring even though she's a widow.

"I'll see you both later," Aunt Sylvia says.

"Thank you for the ride," Jai says.

"You're very welcome," Aunt Sylvia says. Behind Jai's back, she gives me a massive thumbs-up. God, she's almost as bad as Mom, fangirling over Jai. It seems that in this short space of time, Jai has charmed my aunt—just as he has charmed me. I smile and watch as Ouma Lettie and Aunt Sylvia leave the room.

"I know this looks like a lot of food," Jai says, "but I'm pretty sure I'm going to finish it all." He taps at what I know to be rock-hard abs. "I'm starving."

"Me too." And that's all we talk about as we scarf down the food.

Ouma Lettie comes in when half the food has already been cleared. She laughs. "I forgot what it's like having two teen-age boys under this roof." She pours herself a cup of coffee. Just then Ouma Lettie's phone rings. She squints as she reads the caller ID. "It's harvest season, so it's been busy, busy, busy around the farm." Ouma Lettie leaves the kitchen to take the call.

When I am full, I pull out my phone and am surprised to find a Wi-Fi signal. This will make Mom extremely happy. I already know that I will have several unread messages waiting for me.

Jai groans. "I'm stuffed."

"Me too," I agree, and get up from the table. "Coffee?"

"Please." He nods. "I feel like I'm running on fumes."

I pour Jai and myself some coffee. Jai takes his black; I need milk in mine.

I walk to the fridge, and my eyes snag on the papers that are attached to the door with magnets. The itinerary that Aunt Sylvia mentioned in the car is there. And aside from other reminders for Ouma, I see a note with the Wi-Fi password. *Score!*

"Ouma, is it okay if Jai and I use the Wi-Fi?" I ask once Ouma has returned to the kitchen.

Ouma nods as she rifles through some drawers before leaving again. I read the password out to Jai and connect to the internet. Just like I thought, I have no fewer than ten messages from Mom.

> I already miss you!

> Can I survive two weeks without you:(

> I can't find my keys! Help!!!!

Regardless of the time difference, I text Mom to let her know that I'm safe and sound and with Ouma Lettie now.

Jai's scrolling on his phone too. "Is your mom as worried as mine?" I ask as I take my seat again.

Jai nods. "She's gonna be relieved to hear from me."

"I'm glad she allowed you to come," I say. Our eyes meet. "Thanks for doing this. For coming with me."

"Enough with the thanks," Jai says. "I wanted to do this. I'm happy to be here." Jai pauses before adding, "With you."

Before I can say anything, Jai yawns and continues, "Though right now I'm more tired than anything."

"When you boys are done, I'll show you to your rooms. You can shower and get some sleep," Ouma Lettie says from the next room. Her eyesight may be bad, but her hearing is just fine.

At this moment, nothing in the world sounds better than sleep. I down my coffee faster than I should and scald my tongue. Small sacrifices for a shower and a bed.

Ouma Lettie returns just as we're putting our dishes in the sink. "Leave them," she says. "You two have a free pass today."

We get our bags, and the three of us walk up the stairs. Ouma comes to a stop in front of two doors. She points at the one on the right and says, "Nate in here," and then points to the one on the left. "Jai in here. Fresh linens and towels are on the beds. The bathroom is just next door. I'll be downstairs if you need anything." Her phone rings once more, and she answers it as she leaves.

"You should shower first," I say to Jai.

"Cool, thanks." Jai walks into what'll be his room for the duration of our stay.

I look into mine before stepping inside.

Without having to be told, I know this is Dad's bedroom.

Or it *was*.

12

I enter the room and drop my luggage at the foot of the bed. The room is big but feels cozy. It fits a large bed and, opposite it, a desk. In the corner there's a guitar case. We have one of Dad's at home still. This must be the one he used as a teenager. I do a 360-degree turn and take in the space. All around, little pieces of the man I owe half my existence to stare back at me.

It seems that Ouma Lettie hasn't changed much of the room since Dad moved out. It looks stuck in time. And I guess maybe that's what death is like, a person's life being put on pause . . . forever.

I'll explore and snoop later, but for now I just take a mental picture.

I hear the shower start in the next room. I throw myself onto the bed, and my stiff muscles scream with joy as I sink into the soft mattress. While I wait for Jai to be done in the shower, I pull out my phone. I ignore the low-battery warning and scroll through Instagram. Due to the time difference, everyone's posts are from a few hours before.

I must doze off, and Jai startles me awake when he comes into the bedroom, drying his hair with a towel.

"I'm all done," he says. I blink at him a few times, trying to get my bearings, which makes him laugh. He throws the towel over his shoulder and pulls me by the arm, trying to get me to stand. "Shower first, then sleep."

I shake my head. My body's dead weight. Jai pulls more forcefully and trips over the rug.

"Aaah!" Jai screams as he hops and then, somehow, lands on top of me. *Oh, God!*

We're face to face, chest to chest. I blink—slowly—and he does too.

Okay, I'm fully awake now.

Blood rushes both north to my cheeks and south to my— *Uh-oh!*

"Getting up now!" I say a little too loudly. We scramble apart from each other. Jai clears his throat. He's nervous, I realize. I am too.

Is this the right time? *Maybe I should tell him I like him,* I think. Yet the words stay lodged firmly in my throat.

I wish I were braver than I am. Before I can muster up an ounce of courage, Jai breaks the silence.

"Uh, good night," Jai says. We both turn to look out the window at the bright sunshine. "I mean, morning." He turns to me with a smile on his face. I mirror it—though mine is more nervous than his. I know I will scold myself later for missing this opportunity.

"I'll see you in a few hours" is all I can say.

I watch Jai leave. I look down. *This is going to be a problem,* I think. I take a few calming breaths and collect my stuff for the bathroom. Once I'm in the shower, I open the cold tap for a few moments and let the freezing water calm me down.

I want Jai Patel.

I have wanted him for a long time.

And I just got the feeling that he wants me too.

I wake up several hours later. It feels like I'm emerging from the depths of the ocean. Slowly I blink back into reality. It takes me a moment to remember that I am in South Africa.

I grab my phone on the bedside table, only to find a dead screen staring back at me. I groan as I reach for the charger.

When my phone flashes on, I reply to a message from Mom and then turn my attention to the fifty-plus messages in the band group chat. I think nothing of it at first, because the band loves to share memes and links to videos and stuff. It's only as I scroll down that I realize it is a state of emergency. That we, as the band, are screwed six ways from Sunday.

Thorn released a new song.

They released *our* new song.

"Alone" is the song that Infinite Sorrow has been practicing for Ready2Rock.

I pull my phone off the charger and head to Jai's room. I open the door to find our fearless leader dead asleep.

"Jai?" I call out. He doesn't hear me.

"Jai," I say, louder this time. He grumbles and turns over.

"Jai, wake up!" Startled, he sits up and yawns. "You need to look at your phone."

"What?" Jai's hair sticks up in every direction. It looks like a bird's nest. *Cute*, I think, before remembering the very big issue at hand.

"Look at your phone," I repeat.

He seems confused for a moment. And then, like a switch has been flipped, he's fully awake.

"What the fuck," Jai curses. He springs from the bed, and— Oh, boy.

Jai sleeps in his boxer briefs. It's something I've recently learned, thanks to him sleeping over on the eve of the trip, and yet I am not at all ready for the sight in front of me.

Right now I am but a humble teenage boy ruled by hormones.

"Nate?" Jai asks. I look up from his . . . one, two, three, four, five, six abs and meet his dark gaze. He's been talking to me, but I haven't heard a single word he has said. *God, I need to stop perving.* As he pulls on a shirt, I force myself to look only at his face.

"I can't believe Ross did this," I say.

"I should have punched him when I had the chance to," Jai grumbles. He sits on the bed and sends a message in the group chat. Then he searches for the song online and plays it.

It is our song.

I sit down next to him and read some of the comments over his shoulder.

Thorn is fire.

What's the new singer's Insta? <3 Asking for a
friend . . .

They're going to win Ready2Rock.

Everyone loves "Alone." They love our song, and yet it isn't ours anymore. It's Thorn's.

"It's over," Jai says. He throws his phone beside him and buries his face in his hands. This is not how our trip is supposed to be going, and we can't even fix this. We're literally an ocean away from the rest of the band—on a different continent. The competition is in three weeks. We don't have time for such a massive disaster.

"We can't let them win," I say. I've wanted to beat Ross from the very beginning, but what was once a spark is now a mighty inferno. There's nothing that I hate more in this world than cheaters—and "Stupid Love" by Lady Gaga.

"We have nothing," Jai says. "We need a new song for the competition. It's a rule." Our set for Ready2Rock has to consist of three songs—two from our catalog and a brand-new one. The rules specify that a song is considered new if it's unreleased or if it's been released in the current year. So, Thorn and Ross timed their scheme perfectly.

I turn to him. "Then we write one. You and I."

Jai looks up at me. "There's not enough time."

"We're both damn good songwriters," I remind him. "Lorde wrote 'Royals' in thirty minutes when she was our age. We can do this." I raise my fist in what is meant to be a cheer-like gesture.

Even though he doesn't want to, Jai smiles.

"You remember the exact details of Lorde writing 'Royals'?" Jai asks. "You just woke up."

"I'm always thinking of the brilliance that is Lorde," I say matter-of-factly. I'm being very serious, and yet Jai laughs until his eyes start to tear up.

Then he rests his head on my shoulder. I tense for a heart-beat and force myself to calm down.

"Thanks," Jai says. I feel him breathing.

"For what?" I'm confused. And excited. Scared. Nervous. Anxious. All of the above.

"For making me laugh," Jai says.

"I was being serious," I say.

"I know," Jai says. He pulls back from my shoulder and rests his forehead against mine. My heart speeds up. "You always know how to make me feel better. Even at times like this, when everything feels like shit, you make me happy."

For a moment I wonder if he'll kiss me. But then he pulls back, to my disappointment. I've wanted to kiss Jai Patel for a very long time.

"So how do we do this?" Jai asks. "Where do we even start?"

He's now all business. This is Jai Patel, the leader of Infinite Sorrow. So I try to focus on the matter at hand too. Even though I am totally distracted by what just happened. Damn, if this is how the two weeks with Jai are going to go, I don't think my heart or I will survive it.

"Well, we don't have to start from scratch," I say.

"What do you mean?" Jai asks.

"We have the song I heard in your car. The one you've been working on."

"That song isn't near being ready," Jai says. "It was just me messing around."

"Still, it's something. Besides, we can make it ready. Then when we get back home, we'll teach it to the rest of the band and practice all we can." I take his hand in mine. "We can do this."

"You really think so?" Jai looks down at our clasped hands.

"I do," I say.

He's silent for a moment—thinking.

"Then let's do this," Jai says.

"Yes, let's," I say.

And I can't help but think of all the other things I would like to do with Jai.

13

I did not expect my morning to start with being chased by a gaggle of geese, and yet here I am, being chased by a loud and angry gaggle of geese.

It wasn't really my choice. I came down for breakfast, and Ouma Lettie asked me to collect some fresh eggs. I'd walked halfway to the chicken coop when I was spotted by Thanos and his gang. Thanos is the name I've given to their leader. The angriest and fastest of the geese—the one that is currently trailing right behind me.

"Get away from me, you stupid goose!" Thanos doesn't listen. Nor do the rest of them. So I have to keep running. Round and round in circles.

I hear someone laughing and look at the porch, where Jai is standing. "You okay?"

"Do I look okay?" Do geese bite? I'm not sure of the answer, but I'd rather not find out, thank you very much. I'm not super athletic—and by that I mean at all—but damn it, I will not lose to these glorified chickens.

"What did you do to make them so angry?" Jai asks. He's

put down his cup of coffee and is walking toward me. A goose spots him, and Jai freezes.

"I don't know," I say. "I was just walking, and Thanos decided to attack me."

"Thanos? You had the time to name it?" Jai asks.

"I'm a man of many talents," I say.

"What can I do to help?" Jai asks. He looks from me to the monster that is eyeing him.

Just then Ouma Lettie comes out. "What's all the fuss about?" she asks before taking in the scene. "Oh, those bastards are at it again."

"Ouma!" I scream. Relief floods my body. "Help me."

"There isn't anything I can do," Ouma Lettie says. "You have to stand still."

"What!" I want to stare at her in disbelief, but I can't. I cannot stop. I will not stop and become bird food. Yes, I know that they aren't carnivores, but let's see how much everyone cares about biology when they're being chased by an army of feathered fiends.

"That's the only way to get them to stop," Ouma Lettie says.

"No, no, no, no," I chant as I do another lap around the yard.

"Just get it over with, Nate!" Jai calls.

"That's easy for you to say." I refuse. I will run until I can't anymore.

"Nate, just do it!" Jai says. "On three."

"One." *Oh God, oh no!*

"Two." *Am I really going to do this?*

"Three." *Shit, I am. I do.*

I freeze, and Thanos plucks away at me. Then the rest do too. I want to scream and fight, but Ouma Lettie stops me.

"Don't act hostile to them. It only makes it worse. Try to stay calm, and it'll be over soon," she says.

I'm not sure how long I'm attacked, but I cower with my hands over my head. I grit my teeth in pain. Until it's over.

I startle at a touch. I chance a peek and find Jai standing over me. "It's okay," he says. "You survived."

He pulls me up by the hand and examines me. "You okay?" he asks.

"I was just attacked by murderous geese," I say. "That is an actual thing that has happened to me in my life."

Jai chuckles. "Who knew farm life was so dangerous, huh?"

"You remind me of your father," Ouma Lettie says from the porch. "Geese were his sworn enemies." She laughs. "And sheep."

"Sheep?" I ask.

"He was once kicked by one when he was young. After that he would avoid them," Ouma Lettie explains.

"I mean, I understand him. I'm pretty sure I never want to see those monstrous birds again," I say.

"Did you get the eggs?" Jai asks.

"No, I hadn't grabbed them yet."

"Come on—I'll help you," Jai says.

I look around slowly. "You don't think I'll be attacked again, do you?"

"I'll be your shield this time," Jai says. He bumps me with his hip. "Come on."

"Are you trying to be the hero?" I ask.

"Maybe."

We walk toward the chicken coop. And as we do, I keep an eye out for Thanos and his gang, but we don't see them again. When the chickens spot us, they make a loud ruckus.

"So how do we do this?" Jai asks.

"Ouma Lettie said we go in there and just take them," I say.

Jai and I pause for a minute to watch the chickens before turning to each other.

"How, exactly, do we just go in there?" I ask.

Jai shrugs. "Beats me."

God, two city boys on a farm—what could go wrong, right?

"One of us just needs to open the door and go in," I say.

"Who?" Jai asks. "Me?"

"You did want to be the hero," I say. "Now's your chance."

Jai squints at me for a moment before sighing. "Fine," he says. "We can't let you get attacked by chickens too."

"Your sacrifice is noted," I say.

Jai reaches for the door latch. After a calming breath, he opens the door and enters the coop. He is careful to close the door behind him. We really don't need the chickens to escape. I am most certainly not in the mood to do any more running this morning. I've had my fill.

Jai pauses and studies the chickens as they stare back at him. A while later he takes a step forward and then another. They're totally unbothered by him. Jai manages to collect five eggs with ease.

"Well, that was simple," I say.

"Yeah," Jai says. "I'm actually kind of embarrassed to admit how scared I was before."

"Me too." I look at him. "How about we never ever speak of this again?" I hold up a pinky. "Deal?"

Jai hooks his pinky with mine. "Deal."

I cradle the eggs as we walk back. "How are you feeling?" I ask. "About Ross?" We may have found a solution for the competition. But before he was a bandmate, Ross was Jai's friend. His betrayal is a deep cut.

"It just feels like I really didn't even know him, you know?" Jai shakes his head. "Besides you and Gemma, Ross was the next person I would actually consider a best friend."

"I still can't believe what a flaming asshole he is," I say.

Jai laughs. "That's a new one."

"Sorry." The "flaming" was on account of his red hair—you get the picture. No disrespect to other redheads.

"No, he is." Jai sighs. "Him leaving the band hurt, but in a way, I understand. He had his reasons. And with time, I think we could've gone back to being friends. But there is no going back from this. What Ross did is low and dirty."

"You're right. People like Ross will always get what they deserve," I say. It is something I've always believed—that the universe has to be fair. That mean and bad people will eventually face the consequences of their actions. There just has to be a balance, you know?

"I only hope we can pull this off," Jai says. "A brand-new song in two weeks."

"We've got this," I say. I hold my hand up for a high five and almost end up dropping one of the eggs that I'm carrying.

"Maybe we should 'get it' after breakfast," Jai teases.

"That sounds like a plan."

We head into the kitchen and hand the eggs to Ouma Lettie.

"You boys should wash up. Breakfast will be ready in a few."

Jai and I go upstairs. I use the bathroom first. When I'm done washing my hands, I stop to examine my injuries from the vicious goose attack. Aside from a few red spots on my legs, I'm mostly fine. My body is still sore, which is more annoying than it is painful.

If only Mom could see me now. She's always said I have a tendency to be overly dramatic when I get hurt. I'll be the first to admit that I do not like pain. I mean, who does? There is nothing wrong with being *slightly* dramatic.

"Stop checking yourself out in the mirror," Jai teases from the doorway. "You always look good."

I turn to him. "Are you flirting with me?" *Mm-kay, that was a tad too forward. Retract, retract.*

After a pause, Jai says, "Yeah, I am," in a tone that makes it seem like it's not a big deal.

But it is.

He turns and walks away, leaving me and my pounding heart to deal with the aftermath of what he just said.

Is he joking? He has to be joking, I assure myself.

14

Ouma Lettie has farm stuff to deal with, so Jai and I are left to our own devices for the rest of the day. Our bodies still aren't used to the change in time zone, so we both opt for a quick nap before we start working on the song.

I'm in my room—my dad's room—staring at the bookshelf in the corner. There's a big selection of novels. I'm surprised to find no dust when I trace their spines. Ouma Lettie must clean here often.

I grab a book, *Cry, the Beloved Country* by Alan Paton, and flip through the pages. They are yellow from age, and many of them have been dog-eared. A few passages are highlighted as well. Mom always said Dad was a bookworm. One of the things she used to love was listening to him read his favorite passages aloud. Mom also said that the first time she laid eyes on Dad, he had his nose buried in a book. Later she saw him playing guitar, and she knew then and there that she would marry him.

I hold on to the book and scan the rest of the items on the shelves. There's a gold figurine of a goalie, and my dad's name is engraved on its base. VINCENT HARGREAVES. That's him, my father.

I had no clue my dad had played soccer. This proves that my lack of athletic ability is thanks to Mom and not Dad. It's funny how this small detail feels like a puzzle piece of myself that I never knew was missing.

My eyes snag on a photo album, and I pull it free. I move over to the bed and start to flip through the snapshots of my dad's youth. Staring at a picture of him when he was my age, I can see the resemblance that Mom talks about so often. I study the lines of his face and smile.

I turn the pages. There's a family shot of Ouma Lettie, Uncle Richard, and the two now-gone members of their family. My grandfather died way before I was born.

A photo falls free as I near the last page. It's of Mom and Dad when they were much younger. Dad's arm is draped over Mom's shoulder, and she's beaming into the camera. They're seated in some field, maybe a park, and Dad has his guitar near him. I really got into music because of Dad. I guess in a way I wanted to get close to him.

They look happy and in love. Who knew Mom would have so few years left with her soul mate? She's lived on from this picture. She has wrinkles now and gray streaks in her hair—proof of her life. Her smile now is different from the one here. She smiled with excitement. Now she smiles with experience.

I snap a photo with my phone. Mom and I don't really talk about Dad, and I'm not sure if she'll appreciate what I'm about to do. But before I can second-guess myself, I send her the picture.

I add a caption: *Mom and Dad*, with a heart.

I'm still staring at the photo when Jai enters the room. He puts his guitar down at the foot of the bed before sitting next to me. "Who's that?"

"My mom and dad when they were younger." I look up at him.

"Wow. They're stunning," Jai says. "I see where you got your looks from."

I smile. "This is the first time I've really seen our resemblance. Dad's and mine."

Jai throws his arm over my shoulders and I lean into his warmth. We look through the album together, and I'm so glad that he is here with me.

I gesture toward the guitar. "I thought you wanted to nap?"

"I tried," Jai says. "But it's like my brain and body want two different things, so I came to check if you were free."

Before I can answer, Jai reaches for his guitar and starts to strum a tune. With the moment gone, I turn to focus on the song he's playing. But halfway through, I get distracted by Jai. He must feel my eyes on him, because he looks up and our eyes crash into each other.

He misses a chord and I laugh. "Nervous?" I tease.

"Well, yeah. You're looking at me like *that*."

"Like what?" I ask, feigning innocence.

Jai plays a bit of the melody as we try to figure out the rest of the song.

"Maybe we should change the key," I suggest. "I think this will be too high for me."

"I think you can do it," Jai says. "We'll try it out when we get some lyrics down for this part."

I clear my throat. "Are you sure?"

Jai smiles and starts the song from the top. For now we're focusing on the melody. Lyrics will come later.

After messing with the tune for a while, I shift in my seat and end up nudging him with my elbow. Jai misunderstands my mistake as a game and nudges me back. I'm never one to back down from a challenge.

"You know you can't win," I say.

Jai snorts and places his guitar down. "Let's see what you've got, then."

He tackles me to the ground, and we roll around on the rug.

"Ouch, rug burn!" I exclaim.

"Sorry," Jai starts to say, but as he moves to pull himself up, I grab his wrists and manage to get the advantage.

"All is fair in love and war, my friend." My smugness is short-lived, though. Because almost effortlessly Jai flips me over and pins me down.

"Cheater," he says.

I struggle to get up but fail. Jai used to be an athlete, after all.

"I win," Jai announces. Now it's his turn to be smug.

We're both breathing heavily now.

With Jai on top of me, I can't help but wonder who the true winner really is.

"I don't think the creative juices are flowing today," Jai says. He gets off me. "I can't concentrate."

"Yeah," I say, sitting up. "We are clearly no Lorde."

Jai laughs. "Well, if we were musical prodigies, we probably would've had hit number one singles by sixteen too." He stands with his guitar. "I'm going to head back to my room."

When he leaves, I pull out my phone.
Mom replied to the photo I sent her.

💜 I'm so glad you're there.

Me too. Love you mom.

Love and miss you, Sonno.

A yawn later, I throw my phone on a pillow and get under the blanket.

———

Ouma Lettie orders takeout for dinner.

"I got us Nando's," she says as she places the shopping bags of food on the table. The smell instantly hits us, and now I'm starving.

"Nando's? What's that?" I ask.

"Do you not have Nando's in America?" Ouma Lettie looks at me like I've just told her that Santa isn't real.

"Not in California," I say. "I've never heard of it."

"It's chicken," Jai says.

"How do you know?" I ask.

"I had it when I went to England. It's amazing."

How amazing can it be? I wonder with a drumstick in hand. A bite in, I get my answer.

What is this sorcery?

I can't focus on anything else but the pieces of chicken that are calling me like a siren song. I'm clearly under some sort of spell, because before I know it, I'm looking down at a plate of just bones. My life will now forever be divided between two versions of me: Nate before Nando's and Nate after Nando's.

"I am a changed man," I whisper to Jai.

He laughs. "I told you it was good."

We help Ouma Lettie with the cleanup. When we're done, Jai and I move to the porch, where the sunset has painted the hills ocher. I take a seat on the wooden swing, and Jai sits down on the steps. He has his guitar with him.

Roscoe and Coco lie at his feet, and Jai welcomes them with scratches on their necks. After a while he starts to strum away, and I open the book I brought down from my bedroom.

"Sylvia just phoned," Ouma Lettie says, walking out the door. She joins me on the porch swing. "It seems we're having a braai tomorrow. Richard wants to spend time with his nephew. So it looks like I'll have to wait another day before putting you two strong boys to work."

"I don't think I'll be very good at farm life," I admit.

"I'm all for it," Jai says. "When else will we ever be able to say we worked on a farm in South Africa?"

Ouma Lettie laughs. "I hope you don't lose all that enthusiasm for the farm work." She takes a sip of her tea before turning to me. "You know you can stay with the other guests if you want. I'm not sure if it's your mom making you, but you don't have to spend time on the farm. You could start having the full wedding experience. I'm sure that'd be more fun than spending time with this old lady."

"I want to be here," I say. "With you."

With Dad.

Ouma Lettie smiles. I lean back and lay my head on her shoulder. After that, we sit in silence, a comfortable one. With Jai strumming out a ballad, we watch the African sun set.

Today was a good day.

My heart is full.

15

The next day, Jai and I are on the porch working on the new song.

"The song is called 'Run,' and it's about someone wishing to run away from all the bad things in his life," Jai explains. "It's a fantasy for that person who wants to escape because their life is a mess and everything just feels too hard. In the end, though, they have to stay, because leaving isn't always an option."

"But the desire to go still remains," I add.

Jai stops petting the dogs and turns to me. "Exactly," he says with a big smile. "That's exactly it."

I tap the side of my head. "We're on the same wavelength."

Jai laughs. "Clearly." He picks up his guitar and starts to play. "So I have a rough chorus for the song," Jai says. "That's the bit you heard in the car that day."

Jai sings as he plays: *"I want to run / Get away faster than you can catch me / I want to run / Far away, where no one can tame me / Run, run, run away / Live my life on the run / I'm chasing my dreams and no one can stop me / So I'll run."*

"Now we just need the rest of it," I say.

"Sounds easy enough," Jai says with a snort. All the while, he plays the music that he has already worked out. The tempo is slow before speeding up.

"Since this is about someone wanting to run away because things are too hard, we should open with a line about that. 'When it gets hard, and I can't cope'?" I shake my head. That seems too on the nose. I close my eyes and listen to the music again. "When it gets dark out, and I'm alone . . ."

Jai sings the line over the melody.

"I dream of finding a place like home?" I add.

Jai repeats the two lines over and over again. "That sounds okay for now." He nods his agreement.

"We should—" I begin to say, but I'm interrupted by the sound of the gate to the farm opening. A silver pickup is driving in, and as it gets closer, I recognize the driver. It's Uncle Richard.

Uncle Richard is tall, with brown skin, a goatee, and a bald head. Even though there was a gap in age between Uncle Richard and Dad, they were always close. They also looked alike. Mom says people often thought they were twins.

All along I've been nervous about seeing Uncle Richard. I haven't seen him since I came out.

"Hi, Uncle Richard," I say as he gets out of the Toyota. I show off the full smile that my orthodontist and six years of braces gave me.

"Nate, it's so good to see you," he says.

My smile falters. "You too," I whisper, disappointed. Usually, he would pull me into a quick hug. It's how he's always greeted me, but today is different.

Is it because he now sees *me* as different?

No, it can't be. He sounds the same. It's just because Jai's here with me.

As if to prove my point, Uncle Richard turns to Jai. "And this is?" he asks. I analyze his tone, searching for any hints that something has changed.

"My best friend Jai," I respond. My voice comes out softer than usual—unsure.

I'm totally overthinking this.

"It's nice to meet you, sir," Jai says, and holds out his hand to Uncle Richard, who doesn't miss a beat and shakes it.

"A lot can be said about a man's handshake," Uncle Richard replies with a big grin. "A strong, good-looking boy like you must have all the girls in the palm of his hand. Do you have a girlfriend, Jai?"

"No, sir, I don't," Jai says.

"Not to worry. Those things come in time." Uncle Richard turns to us. "Can you boys help me unload the bakkie?" He heads over to his pickup truck, or bakkie, and we both follow suit. We grab a cooler box filled with today's ingredients. There are packs of steaks, chops, and sausages as well as some carrots, onions, potatoes, corn, and broccoli.

Uncle Richard pulls out a braai stand—a grill of sorts—and a very large three-legged cauldron, which is a must for cooking a potjie. It looks like the kind a witch would use to brew potions.

Jai and I are grabbing the braai stand when Ouma Lettie comes out of the house.

"Hey, Ma," Uncle Richard says as he gets a bag of charcoal and places it on the ground.

"Hi, son," Ouma Lettie says as she scans everything that Uncle Richard has brought. "You came prepared. We're having both a braai and a potjie—you're spoiling us."

Uncle Richard nods. "Just missing a table and chairs. Do you still have that camping stuff from a few years ago?"

"Yes. It should still be in the shed," Ouma Lettie says. "You know where the keys are."

"Could you give me a hand . . . Jai?" Uncle Richard asks.

"Sure," Jai says. I stare at Uncle Richard, but he seems to be looking everywhere but at me. I turn to Jai and Ouma Lettie, who seem unbothered. Again, I'm sure I'm just feeling sensitive today.

When Uncle Richard returns from the storage shed, he busies himself with starting the fire. We're a few feet away from the porch as Jai sets up the table before going over to help my uncle. Soon they have a whole system going.

"Do you need me to do anything, Uncle Richard?" I ask.

"No, I think Jai and I have got it handled." My uncle doesn't even bother looking at me.

I stand there awkwardly.

"Jai, could you grab me some more coal?" Uncle Richard asks.

I turn to look for Ouma Lettie, but she's gone back into the house. I find her in the kitchen. "What are you doing?" I ask.

"I'm making potato salad," Ouma Lettie says. She puts the eggs and potatoes into a pot to boil. After that she scans the kitchen with her lips pursed. "Nate, can you get me two tins of baked beans, please?"

I nod and get the cans from the cupboard. "What are you doing with these?"

"I'm going to make a baked bean salad. Richard likes it," Ouma Lettie says. "But your father used to *love* it. We couldn't have a braai without it."

"Baked bean salad. I didn't know Dad loved it," I say, excited to try one of Dad's favorites.

"It's a simple recipe. Just open the can of baked beans and pour it into a bowl. Add some chopped chilies, diced onion, and tomato, and then mix it all together with some mayonnaise." Ouma prepares the food as she explains each step.

In the end, I'm not much of a help, save for washing the dishes.

When we walk outside, we find that Jai and Uncle Richard have moved the potjie pot onto the fire, and the broth is cooking away. Potjie is a stewlike dish that has to be cooked outdoors in a three-legged cauldron.

"I missed a FaceTime from Mom, so I'm going to go return the call," Jai tells me as I grab a chair. His hair is up in a ponytail, and there's a streak of soot on his cheek. Without thinking, I reach for his face and wipe off the smudge.

I look around and find Uncle Richard staring at us. His face is serious, the smile from before gone. Well, this is awkward. A moment later, he starts talking to Ouma Lettie.

"Thanks," Jai says.

I clear my throat. "No problem."

Jai walks into the house, leaving me alone with Ouma

Lettie and Uncle Richard. We're standing in front of the braai stand and the potjie pot. The heat from the fire warms the air.

"I usually prefer a potjie with tripe—black tripe, to be specific," Uncle Richard says as he lifts the cauldron lid and stirs the mixture. "But I wasn't sure if you'd like it, so we're using beef bones today." Uncle Richard keeps his eyes focused on the pot before him.

"Tripe?" I ask. "As in . . ."

"Animal intestines," Ouma Lettie says. "Or matumbu." She sees the grimace that crosses my face, and she laughs. "I think you made the right call leaving out the tripe," she tells my uncle.

"At least this way we don't have to deal with swarms of flies that come with cooking tripe," Uncle Richard says. He moves over and uses a stick to push the coals in the braai stand. "The fire's just right now."

Ouma Lettie and I watch as Uncle Richard throws the meat on the grill. It sizzles.

Jai returns then.

"I think I brought too much meat," Uncle Richard says. "Luckily, Jai looks like a young man with an appetite."

"It isn't just him," Ouma Lettie says. "Nate eats a lot too. More than you and Vincent used to at their age. If these two were staying longer than two weeks, I'd worry about being eaten out of the house."

Uncle Richard pats his slightly protruding belly. "Oh, to be young."

"We both know that's a beer boep," Ouma Lettie says. "You drink too much of that stuff. You'll end up with gout, like your father."

"There's nothing better than braaied meat and an ice-cold beer." Uncle Richard watches the meat on the braai for a moment before taking a deep breath. "This is the smell of South Africa," he says.

And it's the taste of South Africa too. Braaied meat is like barbecue, but because of the braai spices that Uncle Richard has added, the meat has layers of flavor that I haven't tasted before. This stuff is gold.

By the time we're finished eating the braai meat, it's finally time to taste the potjie. While we were eating, the sun started to set, and now dusk surrounds us. Even here on this farm, the wide-open golden fields and abundance of trees and nature are astonishing.

"We can just have a taste now, and you can eat the rest tomorrow," Uncle Richard says.

"You're saving me from cooking," Ouma Lettie says. "I was just now trying to figure out what to make."

Uncle Richard scoops the brown gravy of the potjie into our bowls. He makes sure each of us gets some vegetables and meat too. The taste of potjie is hard to describe. It's thicker and richer than normal stew somehow, but I know that I'd never be able to explain it to anyone.

By the time the meal ends, I've given up trying to analyze Uncle Richard's every word and action. Jai and I help take the plates back into the kitchen. By then it's already nighttime, and we finish packing everything away by the headlights of the pickup truck.

"I'll see you this weekend, right?" Uncle Richard asks.

I nod. Uncle Richard closes the space between us. I tense

up, but he grabs me into the hug that I've been waiting for all day. Relief crashes into me like a tidal wave.

As he pulls away, I can't hide my smile.

"Great," Uncle Richard says. "It was nice meeting you, Jai. I'll see you ous later."

As Uncle Richard leaves, so does my anxiety. The knot that formed in my stomach loosens up. I sigh and look up at the night sky.

Far away from all the city lights, a curtain full of stars hangs above us. It's a picture-perfect image that artists throughout history have tried to capture, but nothing quite lives up to the real thing.

I don't know why I even worried about seeing Uncle Richard. He's clearly cool. Nothing has changed between us, and that makes me happy.

Everything is fine.

16

The next morning, Meghan arrives in a fire-engine-red sports car that has absolutely no business driving on farm roads. And yet my cousin is totally unbothered by this.

The lifestyle of the filthy rich should only be looked at from afar and without the hope of being understood. It's a lesson I learned pretty early on from spending time with Meghan. She's never really had to think about money. Whether that's good or bad I don't really know. And who am I to judge, anyway? All I can say is that she is blessed to live as she does.

Meghan makes a show of getting out of the car. Everything about my cousin is dramatic—and that is saying something, coming from me. I always thought she would do well as an actress, but Meghan likes math and science. Despite being several years older than me, she has always been my ride or die.

"Nathaniel!" Meghan squeals as she envelops me in a very tight hug. My cousin insists on calling me that because, according to her, I'm an old soul and need to learn how to live a little. Over the years I've given up trying to argue with her.

"Hey, Meg," I say into her shoulder. She is wearing a dress

that looks like a sack with polka dots, but I'm sure this very garment was sent down some runway in some city designated the fashion capital of the world.

Meghan pulls away and looks at Jai. "When Mom said you brought your boyfriend, I had to come see him for myself." She taps her designer shades so that they now rest on the bridge of her nose and gives Jai a once-over.

"He's not my boyfriend," I say. But both of them ignore my words.

Jai holds out his hand. "Hi, I'm Jai."

Meghan shakes his hand with her perfectly manicured one. "Meghan."

We head inside so Meghan can say hi to Ouma Lettie, and as we do, she whispers into my ear, "Damn. He's cute." Even though I agree one hundred percent, I don't say anything.

"Ouma!" Meghan shouts when we enter the house.

"I'm in the office," Ouma Lettie calls back. Meghan follows her voice.

"So she's the bride-to-be?" Jai asks. He trails after me as I walk toward the kitchen.

"Yup," I say. "She and Ben have been together since high school."

"Is he American or South African?" Jai asks.

"South African. They did the whole long-distance thing while she was in college. I don't know how they did it, but they did, and now here we are," I explain.

"I think with the right person, I'd be able to manage it too," Jai says.

"Manage what?" I fill a glass of water and take a sip.

"The long-distance thing. After senior year," Jai says. I turn to him, and the way he is looking at me makes me choke on the water.

"Excuse me," I say, and wipe my mouth with the back of my hand.

We're looking into each other's eyes without speaking, just breathing. Jai leans in close to me. Our noses are almost touching. Is this the answer I've been waiting for? Are my feelings reciprocated? Is this going to be our first kiss? There are so many questions that I have, and all of them can be answered if our lips touch.

God, I hope he kisses me. I've waited so long for this to happen.

We're a hair's breadth from each other when someone clears their throat. Jai and I jump, and I let out a *Whoa*. Meghan is leaning against the doorframe, and the moment is completely ruined.

"Well, I'm sorry to interrupt," she says, "but we have a full day of fun planned at Gold Reef City."

I feel heat rush to my face. Out the corner of my eye I see Jai run a hand through his hair. It's something he does whenever he's nervous.

"Give me a sec," Jai says. He walks away.

I down the rest of my water and practically jump out of my skin when I find Meghan standing right beside me. She slowly and dramatically opens her purse. I watch, horrified, as she pulls out a strip of condoms.

"Here," she says innocently.

"Jesus Christ, Meghan. What the hell?" God, the embarrassment. I look toward the door for any sign of Jai or Ouma Lettie. At least Meghan waited until Jai had left the room to do this.

"Listen, there was enough sexual tension in this kitchen to start a fire. I wouldn't even need a match," Meghan says. "So take these and do with them what you will."

"We're not going to have sex," I argue. "We haven't even kissed. I'm not even sure if he likes me. We're just friends."

Meghan snorts. "Just friends!" She shakes her head. "Trust me, you and he have a one-way ticket to pound town."

I groan. "Never say 'pound town' again."

Meghan rolls her eyes and shakes the strip of condoms. "Take them, or I'll give them to Jai."

I hear footsteps and grab the condoms. I shove them into my pocket, and Meghan smiles. "Always be safe." She leaves the kitchen, satisfied that her work is done. "I'll be in the car," she calls over her shoulder.

I lean against the counter and take deep breaths. The condoms in my pocket feel heavy, so I flee and head to my room. I bury Meghan's "gift" deep in my luggage.

The scene in the kitchen plays over and over in my head. I need to know what Jai is thinking—what he's feeling. And if Jai doesn't volunteer an answer, then I'll have to find out myself.

If he doesn't make a move, I will let him know how I feel before the end of this trip. It's decided.

We're all piled in Meghan's two-door sports car on our way to meet some of her friends. I feel bad for Jai, who's folded himself in the back seat. I volunteered to be the human pretzel but Jai refused.

"You should have brought a bigger car!" I tell Meghan. I know her family has more cars than I can count on one hand.

"This car goes with my outfit," Meghan says.

"Oh yeah? How?" I ask. "The car is red and you're in"—I study the color of her dress—"I want to say *olive?*"

Meghan snorts. "You are the last person I'd take fashion advice from." She side-eyes me.

"What's that supposed to mean?" I ask, looking down at what I'm wearing. My Assassin's Creed T-shirt is the height of fashion, and I'll be hearing no arguments on the matter.

Meghan laughs and shakes her head. "You're probably the worst-dressed gay guy ever."

"First, that's a stereotype, and second, I'm not a bad dresser." I turn to look at Jai in the back seat. "Right, Jai?"

Jai raises both his hands in surrender. "I plead the Fifth."

"See, Jai agrees with me," Meghan says. "He, on the other hand, looks good."

Jai is in cutoff jeans, sneakers, and a tank top, and he has a cap on backward. "Good" does not even begin to cover it. I grumble and turn my attention to the road ahead.

We're going to Gold Reef City. It's an amusement park with over thirty rides, the Apartheid Museum, a casino, and a Victorian train station–themed cinema complex. According to a billboard we pass on our way, Gold Reef City is PURE JOZI, PURE GOLD.

We're the first to arrive at Gold Reef City.

"I thought you like to be fashionably late?" I tease Meghan.

"You know me. I like to keep you on your toes," she says. I can't argue with that.

"By the way, do you have time for this? Shouldn't you be having, like, a bachelorette party or something?" I ask.

"The bachelorette party is this weekend, in Durban," Meghan says. "But today I wanted to show you and my friends a good time. And everyone loves an amusement park, right?"

"It's no Disneyland, but it'll do," I say. Which is a massive joke, because I've never been to Disneyland.

"*Bitch*," Meghan says. She draws out the word for emphasis. "There is no Disneyland in Africa. When foreigners think of us, they think of lions in the streets, outhouses, and building water wells. . . . I wonder why."

I start to fidget while we wait for Meghan's friends, because I know that Tommy Herron is on his way. I move to stand by Jai, close enough that our shoulders touch. When he feels me beside him, he playfully bumps into me.

"You'll be fine," he whispers. "I'm right here."

Four people show up ten minutes later.

But my eyes home in on Tommy.

Jai's words must have calmed me down some, because as I look at Tommy, I'm not as nervous as I was. But I sure still am angry.

I've gone several days without having to see him. I almost forgot I dreaded this. But the problem with "almost" is that it is never enough. And that's why I am now standing face to face with the boy who broke my heart.

Tommy's eyes widen in surprise at the sight of me. And the reaction thrills me more than it should.

Tommy is tanner than before. He's wearing shorts and a short-sleeved button-down shirt that hugs his muscular body, which is new to me too. Maybe he found the time to work out because he wasn't responding to my texts? All in all, he looks different than he did the last time I saw him.

Who knew that when he left for college he'd leave my life? That it was a stop to our love story instead of a pause.

We had all these grand plans to date long-distance. We dreamed up fantasies of traveling and eventually coming out together. I did the latter without him, and who knew that the former would actually come true.

I've imagined this moment. What I would say to him. What I would do to him. But now that I'm here, there is nothing I want to do. I am frozen. I don't know this Tommy Herron. I haven't known him since he cut me from his life without reason or excuse. Time changes people. I'm not the same as before, and I'm sure he isn't either. And yet my heart still remembers.

I carry the memories of the first boy I ever loved.

I am bitter.

I am angry.

I am hurt.

Jai rests a hand on my shoulder and leans in to whisper, "Are you okay?" He's obviously recognized Tommy from the photos I've shown him.

"Not really," I reply.

"For what it's worth, he keeps staring at you like he's seen a ghost," Jai says.

I, on the other hand, have done everything in my power not to look at him again. Jai adds, "I don't think he knew you would be here. *Asshole*." Hearing that one word from Jai makes me smile. And knowing that Jai is here with me helps.

I am not alone.

You can do this, Nate! I say to myself. *Ignore him. Ignore everything.*

"Let's just ignore him," I say. "I don't want him to stop us from having fun today."

"Sounds like a plan," Jai says. "Let's have fun, then." He winks, and I return a small smile—one that is real, because spending time with Jai makes me happy.

Meghan introduces her friends. Of course, from my Instagram stalking—I mean, research—I already know Erika, Tommy's girlfriend. There's Sasha, a tall Black girl with a bob and a septum piercing, and Brooke, who's white with curly brown hair and glasses. I wave, feigning enthusiasm.

"This is my cousin, Nathan," Meghan says. "And this is Jai."

"It's nice to meet you," Erika says. "I'm Erika, Meghan's friend from college, and this is my boyfriend, Tommy."

Erika is a natural redhead, with some freckles spread across the bridge of her button nose.

"I think Nate knows Tommy," Meghan says.

I bristle. Of course, Meghan remembers that I asked her about Tommy. God, that was stupid of me. She looks at me, and all I can do is shrug. I hate this. I would like to be excluded from this conversation, thank you.

"Oh, you guys know each other?" Erika asks. "How?"

"Tommy is from Wychwood," Jai says. "Like us."

I smile at Jai. I felt like a castaway at sea, and now Jai has thrown me a life jacket.

"Hey, Nate. Long time no see," Tommy volunteers gingerly.

And whose fault is that? I think.

"Good to see you, Tommy," I lie.

"How'd you guys meet?" Jai asks Erika. "At Stanford?"

"Our families are friends. They have been for years," Erika explains. "Even though I'm a few years older, I've always found Tommy cute, and then he came to Stanford too, and as they say, the rest is history."

Meghan turns to me. "You're being awfully quiet, Nate. Something wrong?"

"No, nothing," I lie. I've avoided looking at Tommy all this time. "I just want to get on some rides."

"I want to go on everything," Jai says. He sounds like a kid in a candy store, and I don't blame him.

"Me too," I say. "I love roller coasters."

I try not to think of the last amusement park I went to. It was with Tommy. It hasn't been that long since I threw away the strip of photos that we took at a photo booth there. I will not lose myself to the past. Today I will make new memories—with Jai.

"Ooh la la, you two are so cute," Meghan says, looking at me and Jai.

Tommy seems to disagree, though. He scoffs, and we all turn to look at him.

"What's wrong, babe?" Erika asks.

I stare him down. *Yeah, babe. What's wrong?*

"Nothing," Tommy says. He looks away first. "Enough talking. Let's go."

We all agree to meet by the entrance in a couple of hours, and Erika and Tommy wander off with Brooke and Sasha. I pay them no attention after that. Out of sight, out of mind, and all that. Meghan pulls out her phone.

"I'll catch up with you guys later. I need to talk to Ben," she says. Meghan leaves me and Jai alone.

"How are you feeling?" Jai asks.

"Like I've been shot," I say. "That was harder than I thought it would be."

"You did it. You survived. And now we will have fun and completely forget about that asshat Tommy Herron." Jai turns and points to the swing ride. "How about that first?"

The ride is like a large carousel, but instead of horses, there are swings attached. We watch it spin, sending the riders circling through the air. I quote my favorite Ariana Grande song: "I see it, I like it, I want it."

"Then let's do it," Jai says. He grabs and squeezes my hand in excitement like it is the most natural thing in the world. Today I don't question it. I'm already too emotionally drained.

We get in line for the ride. And when we're buckled in, I have a moment of panic. *Is this safe?* But before fear consumes me, we're sent hurtling through the air, and the only thing I can do then is scream my lungs out.

"Holy shit, that was amazing," Jai says after the ride. "What's next?"

The next ride we settle on is a roller coaster. I take a

moment to pause and watch the people on the ride. The perfectly named Anaconda carries them up, then down, then upside down, and all the while they scream.

I fake choke up. "It's beautiful," I say.

"I'm just glad I didn't overeat this morning," Jai says.

I laugh. "That would have been a disaster."

"That's why we should ride everything we want to before we stop for lunch," Jai says. "I don't really think throwing up is a memory I want to have of this trip."

"Sounds like a plan," I say. It's about a fifteen-minute wait for us to reach the front of the Anaconda line. When we're seated, I reach for Jai's hand.

The roller coaster starts, and so does my screaming. This ride is amazing. And when it ends, Jai and I get back in line. Because one time on a roller coaster is never enough.

After the ride, we head to the meeting spot for lunch. When we arrive, I see that Ben's here. I've met him over Face-Time, and I wave hello.

Ben is tall and handsome, with brown skin and curly black hair. He has a friendly smile on his face.

"What does everyone want for lunch?" Meghan asks.

"Nando's," Jai and I say in unison, and share a smile. We spotted the sign on our way here.

Then I feel a heavy pair of eyes on me. I turn to see Tommy's stormy gaze.

What's his problem?

"Count me in," Ben says.

"Everyone okay with that?" Meghan asks. Erika and

Tommy both nod, as do Brooke and Sasha. I trail after the group, satisfied they made the right decision.

When we get to the restaurant, I sit between Jai and Meghan and opposite Tommy. We order, and while we wait for the food to come, everyone talks. Everyone but Tommy and me, that is.

My second encounter with Nando's chicken is just as amazing as the first. I suck on a bare drumstick bone, my soul filled with so much joy that not even Tommy's glare can bring me down.

After lunch, I'm too full for any adrenaline, so I decide to skip the rides. While Jai looks for a bathroom, I watch a performance of the South African gumboot dance.

All the dancers wear navy overalls and Wellington boots; some boots are embellished with bells that shake and tinkle whenever the dancers stamp their feet to a rhythm of their own making.

"Are you dating *him?*" A voice drowns out the music. It's Tommy.

"That's none of your business," I say. "If you have a girlfriend, why can't I have a boyfriend?"

"Answer me," Tommy demands.

"You don't get to do that," I say. "You don't get to have an opinion on anything about my life. You left me, remember."

"Well, you don't seem awfully cut up about that," Tommy says.

I'm sorry, what? Is he being serious?

I'm about to explode, when Jai approaches. He looks

between the two of us. His face is a stone-cold mask as he levels his gaze on Tommy.

"Is everything okay here?" Jai asks.

"Fine," Tommy says. And his tone is not friendly—at all.

I roll my eyes. Which is the least of the things I would like to do. I just do not have the time or the energy for this. "Let's go, Jai." I don't wait for his response. Instead I simply walk off. It doesn't take long for Jai to chase me down. He grabs me by the wrist and pulls me to a stop.

"Are you okay?" Jai asks. And I feel like he's asked me this a thousand times already.

"I'm fine," I say with a frown.

"You don't look fine," Jai says. He's studying my face with an expression of concern that sends waves of guilt coursing through me. This is not what I want to be feeling after what almost happened between us this morning. Before the son of Satan burst my bubble.

"Can you just leave it alone, please, Jai?" I snap. And I know it's unfair of me to take this out on him. I hate myself for doing it, but I can't help it. I need a moment. This is too much. There's no way I can ignore Tommy Herron.

Dear God, why is this happening?

Jai holds up his hands. "Wow, okay. Backing off." Jai turns on his heel and walks away. I can't do anything but watch him leave. Jai came to South Africa to help me. He did it *for* me, and I've just upset him for no good reason.

In this moment, I hate Tommy Herron.

In this moment, I hate myself too.

17

Jai Patel is giving me the cold shoulder, and I don't blame him. I was an ass to him this afternoon.

Since returning from Gold Reef City, Jai hasn't said a single word to me. We have never really fought before. If he's ever been upset with me, I haven't been aware of it. I hate this.

Jai's in the shower, and I am pacing a hole through the floor in Dad's bedroom. I know I need to apologize. But the words I need to say just aren't coming out right—they never take shape.

Damn it, Nate! This is all so stupid. I knew Tommy would ruin this trip for me. Before Jai was the boy I liked, he was my friend—one of my closest friends, at that—and I cannot let Tommy Herron be the reason for us fighting.

This encounter with Tommy has forced me to admit that I have a lot of unresolved feelings toward him—more than I thought. If I'm ever going to move on from Tommy, this trip is the moment to do it. It's time to face those feelings.

How my first love ended probably messed me up in ways I don't even know. Maybe it's why I'm afraid of opening up with Jai.

My fretting is interrupted by a FaceTime from Gemma. I've only just picked up when she launches into a rant—no hello, nothing.

"Nathan Hargreaves, I cannot believe that you have not called me one single time since you've been in South Africa. Did I not teach you better than that?" Gemma asks.

"Sorry," I say. Huh—it's so simple to apologize for this. "It's been wild."

"Tell me everything," Gemma says. "How's Jai?" She moves her head as if she'll be able to see him. "Where's Jai?"

"In the shower," I say. "We spent the day at an amusement park."

"I'm so jealous," Gemma says.

"How's your internship?" I ask.

"Busy but fun!" Gemma sighs wistfully. "To think I could have been your plus-one."

"You're still my number one, Gemma," I say.

"Always and forever, baby!"

"Who is that?" I hear Gemma's sister ask. "Your boyfriend?"

Gemma looks off-screen at someone who I assume is her older sister, Tori. She rolls her eyes. "I'm talking to Nate."

Tori squashes her face into the camera view. "Hey, Nate," she says. It's been a long time since I last saw Tori. Having been best friends with Gemma for most of our lives, I know her sister well.

Tori, with her icy-blond hair and large green eyes, is the spitting image of her mother, while Gemma looks more like her dad.

"Hi, Tori," I say.

Gemma pushes Tori out of the shot, but Tori retaliates by tickling her.

"Wait, stop. Truce. Truce! Truce! Let me talk to Nate." Gemma is still wheezing when she returns to the screen. She fixes her hair. "Sorry about that," she says. "Where were we?" Gemma answers her own question a moment later, which is something she does. "Right, how are things with 'he who shall not be named'?"

It's one of Gemma's nicknames for Tommy—depending on her mood, she uses either that or "son of Satan."

This is a chance for me to unload and get advice from another one of my friends, but just like with Jai, I'm not sure how to put all that I'm feeling into words. Or maybe I'm just too scared to try.

"Everything's fine," I lie, and luckily Gemma doesn't have a chance to prod any further, because off camera Tori says, "You're going to be late!"

Gemma groans in response. "Listen, Nate. I'm going to be late if I don't kick my ass into gear. I'll talk to you later. Tell Jai I said hey."

"Bye," I say. Gemma ends the call, and I turn my phone off to conserve battery. I find myself staring at my reflection. I am the only one who can deal with this mess I made. I'm mustering up the courage to talk to Jai when I hear a knock on my door.

Jai stands on the threshold, holding his guitar.

"We really need to finish this song," Jai says. "We can't keep delaying it."

I nod. Sometimes avoidance is the best answer. Jai sits

down on the floor with his back against the bed. Almost immediately he starts playing some chords. I guess we won't be talking unless totally necessary.

I don't even bother telling him that Gemma called. Instead I sit down too, careful to keep my distance. Jai places the notebook with the song lyrics between us. During our songwriting session yesterday, we only managed to rework the opening two lines before Uncle Richard arrived.

Jai starts to sing.

"*When it gets dark out, and I'm alone / I dream of finding a place like home.*"

I stare at the open notebook and listen to Jai repeating the opening lines.

"But these demons won't let me / They call me their own," I add. Jai pauses and looks at me for a moment before restarting the song. This time he sings the two new lines I've suggested.

"Instead of 'these,' maybe 'my' will work better," Jai says. He plays it again with that small change, and it does sound better. We reach for the notebook at the same time and our fingers touch. We both pull back.

The vibes between us are so different than they were this morning. We held hands freely. Jai returns to the guitar, and slowly I reach for the pen and paper. I scratch out "these" and replace it with "my."

This time, when Jai starts the song from the top, I sing.

"I think we should land somewhere between the old lyrics and the new ones," I say. "It feels like something's missing."

I stare at the lyrics again.

When it gets dark out, and I'm alone
I dream of finding a place like home
But my demons won't let me
They call me their own

All the while Jai replays the melody of the first verse.

"Oh, how about this?" I say. Jai starts from the top, and I sing: "*When it gets dark out, and I'm alone / I dream of finding a place like home / This lost little boy only dreams of escaping / But my demons won't let me / They call me their own.*"

Jai nods. "It sounds good. Write it down."

"We'll need to tweak these two lines to avoid the repetition of 'dream/dreams,'" I say, and jot down the new lyrics:

When it gets dark out, and I'm alone
I hope to find a place like home
This lost little boy only dreams of escaping
But my demons won't let me
They linger on
This lost little boy only dreams of escaping

Happy with the first verse, Jai and I work our way through the rest of the song, step by step, slowly but surely. And as we work, I can almost fool myself into believing that everything is okay. Almost—because I can still feel the distance between us. It's colder too, every interaction of ours.

After a couple of hours, we have a rough sketch of the song. It still needs some tweaking, but I can tell that Jai is happy with it. I am too.

"I think that's enough for today." Jai yawns. "I'm beat."

I watch him gather his things and stand to leave. I can't let this be it. I won't go to bed with this issue between us unresolved.

"Wait!" I call out to him, too loud. I stand up. Jai pauses at the door and turns to me.

"What is it?" he asks, and his tone isn't what I am used to.

"I'm sorry," I say, looking at his feet. My voice is soft. "I'm sorry about today. I took out my frustration with Tommy on you, and that isn't fair. So I'm sorry, Jai. I really am."

Jai is silent for a while. He nods before heading to his room.

This trip was bringing us closer together than ever before, but tonight we couldn't be further apart. I want to chase after him, to explain what happened again.

I start to go after him—but I stop myself. He deserves his space. I owe him that.

So I throw myself on the bed and open Dad's book.

I reread the same page until I fall asleep.

18

After a crappy night of tossing and turning, I wake up way, way, *way* too early. So instead of lying in bed, I pull on a hoodie and run downstairs to the porch. Ouma Lettie's already seated on the swing.

"Hi, Ouma."

"Oh, dear!" She startles at my presence. "You shouldn't sneak up on an old lady like that." Ouma Lettie rests a hand against her heart.

"Sorry," I say, and sit down next to her.

"Something wrong?" Ouma Lettie asks. "You and Jai haven't looked right since you came back yesterday."

I look at her. "You could tell?"

"Anyone would be able to tell. Did you guys fight?" Ouma Lettie takes a sip from her cup. I've discovered that Ouma Lettie doesn't drink coffee, only rooibos tea. She claims she has more than enough reasons for sleepless nights, so she doesn't need caffeine added to the list.

I chew at my lip. Ouma Lettie studies me for a moment

before standing suddenly. She places her empty teacup on the swing. "Come with me," she says.

"Where to?" I ask.

"There's a place I've been wanting to show you, and now feels like as good a time as any." When she's walked down from the porch, she turns to me. "We can walk and talk."

Ouma Lettie starts marching, cane in hand. She doesn't wait for me, so I chase after her. The sun has just risen, so the farm is still painted in soft pastels. The air is crisp, and I'm thankful that I put on my hoodie before coming downstairs.

I've never gone for a walk so early in the morning before. At this time back home, I'd be on my last dream of the night.

"You don't have to tell me anything," Ouma Lettie says. "Though I will say that I've lived a long life. So who knows. I might be able to share some advice."

I sigh. "It's not that I don't want to tell you—it's just that I don't know where to begin," I admit. And it's true. This is what I'm feeling. I want to tell someone about what I'm feeling. And Ouma Lettie seems like a solid choice, because even though she's family, she's a stranger to my day-to-day life. She's an outsider looking in.

"So where does it start?" Ouma Lettie asks.

My Trouble starts with Tommy Herron. Capital *T* for both.

"Before anyone knew I was gay, I had a boyfriend," I explain. "It was mostly a secret. Only my other best friend, Gemma, knew. His name is Tommy. And he is here. Now."

Ouma Lettie stops walking, and I do too. "What do you mean, *here?*" she asks.

"I mean that he is a guest at Meghan's wedding," I say.

She looks at me, wide-eyed. "How is that possible?"

I laugh without much humor. "That's the question I've been asking myself since I found out that he'd be here. He's dating one of Meghan's friends, Erika. They all go to the same college."

We start walking again. We follow a trail east toward the rising sun, away from all the buildings on the farm.

"What are the odds of that?" Ouma Lettie says. "So what's the problem with you and this Tommy boy?"

"The problem is that we didn't break up. We were going to do the long-distance thing, but the summer before he went off to college he ghosted me," I say.

"Ghosted you?" Ouma Lettie asks. "What does that mean?"

"Oh, right. It means that he stopped answering my texts and returning my calls. He just cut me out of his life without warning," I explain.

"Well, that's an asshole move," Ouma Lettie says. "I already don't like this Tommy boy."

I laugh. "Yeah, well, the problem is that I used to like him a whole lot—too much. And that makes it feel like there's something unresolved between us. Like, I want answers and an explanation, but at the same time I don't, because I don't want to be hurt any more than I have been. And when I saw Tommy yesterday, I felt all this anger bubbling inside me, so Tommy and I had an argument. And I took my frustration out on Jai, who's just been trying to help. The whole reason he's my guest is to help me deal with the Tommy situation, and, like, I know all this, but I still exploded on him. So he's angry with me."

"I understand why Jai is upset," Ouma Lettie says. "I mean, only a great friend would volunteer to come to South Africa for two weeks just to help you deal with your ex-boyfriend."

"I know," I say. "Which is why I feel so terrible. This is all my fault. It's like I'm stuck between my past and my future."

"Your future?" Ouma Lettie asks.

"I like Jai. I like him a lot," I admit.

Ouma Lettie smiles. "Of course you do. He's wonderful." Ouma Lettie seems to have a clear destination in her head. She stops walking once more and turns to me. "But do you also still like this Tommy boy?"

I pause for a heartbeat. "No. I don't think so. I'm over him. I'm sure I like Jai."

"Are you sure?" Ouma Lettie asks. "You hesitated, and that makes me worry."

"It's not that I like him. I just want to know why he broke up with me the way he did. I know that we can never go back to how we were, but I hate that he's ruined my first love. I'm not saying that our relationship wouldn't have ended. I'm now okay that it did. It's just—I would like closure," I say.

"And there you go," Ouma Lettie says. "That's what you need. Closure. We all need it to be able to move on to our next chapter in life, whatever that may be."

"But how do I get that without wanting to punch Tommy in the face?" I ask.

"The only way for you to get any closure is to have a frank conversation with this Tommy. It's the only way that you will be able to move on and have a healthy and successful relationship in the future," Ouma Lettie says.

"I know. You're right," I say. "I guess I'm just scared."

"But first you need to apologize to Jai and maybe explain all this to him. Jai is a great guy, and he'll understand. You should know that, though. You two are friends before anything else." Ouma Lettie takes my hand in hers. "And for what it's worth . . . screw this Tommy boy. I fully support you and hope that it works out between you and Jai."

I can't help but smile. "Ouma." I pull her into a hug.

"Enough of that," she says. "We're almost there." She points at the hill ahead of us, perfectly framed by a few trees. There's a footpath that leads up the raised ground. Ouma Lettie starts to climb, and I reach for her left arm to help her. "Thank you," she says. "Now that I'm older, I don't come here as often as I used to."

"Come where?" I ask. It doesn't take us long to reach the top of the hill.

There's a young jacaranda tree at the very top. And on the trunk of that tree is a bronze plaque.

VINCENT LUKE HARGREAVES, it reads.

"This is where I scattered your father's ashes," Ouma Lettie says. "I wanted to bring you here at least once before you left."

We stand on top of this small hill, and we're able to see the farm stretching out beneath us. The morning light coats the cow pens as well as the sugarcane fields on our left and the cabbage patch on the right.

Tears are welling up in my eyes, and I notice that Ouma Lettie's glasses look foggy too. I take a step and trace the letters of his name—one by one. This is all that remains of Dad.

Tears are rolling down my cheeks now. I turn around and hug Ouma Lettie again. She pats my back lovingly.

"Your father would have been very proud of you," Ouma Lettie says. "He loved you more than anything in this world. And I know that he's watching us right now. Watching you. And when you meet him in heaven one day, he's going to be overjoyed."

I know it isn't real. That it's all in my head. But when I look up, I see Dad. He's leaning against the tree, smiling at me. I see him as he would be if he were alive. The same age as Mom, with crow's-feet at the corners of his eyes and laugh lines around his mouth. He's going gray, just as she is.

Dad, I miss you.

Dad, I love you.

And I can almost hear him say, "*I love you too, Sonno.*"

Ouma Lettie and I spend some time up on the hill before we walk back to the farm. When we return to the house, Jai is at the foot of the stairs. He looks like he just woke up.

I hug Jai, and he seems startled at first—tense. "What's wrong, Nate?"

I shake my head and tighten my arms around him. After a while Jai leans into the hug.

"I'll be in the kitchen making breakfast," Ouma Lettie says behind us. I'd usually worry about showing PDA in front of Ouma Lettie. Not because we're two boys or because of our sexuality or anything like that. It just feels kind of weird to be touchy-feely in front of an elder. But in this moment, I don't care. Besides, Ouma Lettie seems totally unbothered by us.

Jai looks down at me. "Are you okay?"

"More than okay," I say into his shoulder.

Jai holds me for as long as I need to be held without asking any questions.

I know that regardless of what happens between Jai and me, I will always remember this. That he was here with me on the day I saw my dad.

It's a memory that will be carved into the folds of my heart—forever.

19

It's Friday night, and Jai and I are in my room working on the song again when he suddenly stops playing the guitar and turns to me. We've been going over the song for the last four hours, and since our hug yesterday everything seems to be back to normal. Somehow, it even seems better than before.

"Is 'Run' too similar to 'Alone'?" Jai asks. "I was working on both songs at the same time, but Ross liked 'Alone' better." He shrugs. "I mean, he took the stronger song."

"Are you having doubts?" I ask.

He sighs. "I think so." Jai looks at me. "I'm just thinking: what if we wrote something different? Something Infinite Sorrow hasn't done before? A proper rock ballad. Something like . . ."

"A love song," we say in unison.

"What do you think?" Jai asks.

"If you think this is the right decision, then I'm all for it," I say. "Do you think we can pull it off? A love song, I mean?"

Jai chuckles dryly. "I think we'll do just fine."

The next morning, Jai and I are sitting in a business lounge, waiting for our flight to be called. I'm going to be flying first class for the first time in my life. This is a major improvement from the last time Jai and I waited at the airport, before leaving for South Africa. Of course, I was dealing with a severe lack of sleep then. But why bring up the past? This is just so much better.

"I could get used to this," Jai says as he takes a big sip of his Frappuccino.

I nod. "I wonder when I'll be able to experience a business lounge again."

Uncle Richard and Aunt Sylvia sit to our right with their drinks. Uncle Richard is reading a newspaper, and Aunt Sylvia is typing away at her phone. It's just the four of us traveling today. Ouma Lettie opted out of the trip, claiming she'd seen beaches before and didn't need to see any more. Meghan is already in Durban. She flew out yesterday for her bachelorette party.

Jai and I decided this trip will be more than just sightseeing for us. We need to write this song ASAP, so we're calling this weekend "Durban workshop." Hopefully, the sun, the sand, and the beach will provide enough inspiration for us to write a love song.

It's only been twenty minutes since we sat down when we're called to board our flight. The plane is much smaller than the ones used for international flights, but it still has a section at the front for first-class passengers, which is where Jai and I find our seats.

The first thing I notice is the legroom. Who knew flying could be so comfortable?

The flight to Durban takes an hour, so we land at King Shaka International Airport in the blink of an eye. The city is on the east coast of South Africa, in KwaZulu-Natal, one of the country's nine provinces.

The air in Durban is different from that in Johannesburg. It's much more humid here, and the small trek off the plane and into the terminal makes me sweat.

"Nate, over here!" Aunt Sylvia calls after we pick up our luggage. A black SUV is waiting. We'll be staying at the Southern Empress—one of Aunt Sylvia's hotels on the Durban beachfront.

For thirty minutes we see only highway, but everything changes as we near our destination. The air takes on the smell of the ocean, and in the distance the breaking waves echo. Soon we're in the lobby of the hotel, getting our room key cards. Jai and I will be sharing room 303.

"Let's get settled and meet back down here in the lobby," Aunt Sylvia says. We head toward the elevator and reach the floor where we're staying.

"This is it," Jai says as he comes to a stop before the door. I use my key card and the door unlocks. The room has two double beds.

I place my bags on one of the beds and open the curtains. "Look at this view," I say, awestruck. We've been lucky to get one of the rooms that have a beach view. In the distance, the blue water glimmers in the sun.

I put a pair of beach towels and some sunscreen into my backpack. Jai grabs his guitar before we leave our room and head back down to the lobby. Uncle Richard's already there, talking to Meghan.

"Hey, Nate, hey, Jai," Meghan greets us. She's wearing very large sunglasses.

"Hey, Meghan." Jai offers her a warm smile, which she tries to return, but it ends in a grimace.

"What's wrong with you?" I ask.

"My head is killing me," Meghan says. "I think I went a bit too hard yesterday." She rubs her temples. "I was just telling Dad that you guys will be on your own today. The rest of us need time to recover."

I try to hide my smile. I won't be seeing Tommy Herron today.

Aunt Sylvia arrives just then. "This humidity is going to send my hair home," she mumbles, running a hand through her hair.

Meghan must see the look of confusion on my face, even through her very dark glasses, and explains what Aunt Sylvia meant. "Hair going home is a phrase we colored girls use here in South Africa."

Thanks to my research before the trip—and to a Trevor Noah stand-up special—I already knew that South Africans say "colored" to describe mixed-race people. It's an accepted term here, and one of the racial classifications. Even so, I'm still taken aback.

"Our hair 'goes home,'" Meghan continues, "when it gets wet from water, rain, or sweat and returns to its natural state."

I nod.

"Well, I'm off to sleep," Meghan says. "I'll see you all later. Have fun."

Uncle Richard turns to us when Meghan gets into the elevator. "Since Meghan is down and out, I suggest we split up and let you boys do whatever you want to do," he says. "It's no fun being tied down by us old people."

"Yes, go out and have fun," Aunt Sylvia says. "We'll meet back here at six p.m. or so, and we can go out for dinner."

Uncle Richard opens his wallet and hands me a wad of bills. Rand, the currency of South Africa. "You and your friend have a good time," he says with a large grin. "And come find me if you need more."

"Thank you," Jai says.

Jai and I walk out to the street. The ocean is just a few feet ahead of us, and crowds of people dot the sand. We run across the street and step onto the beach.

"I can't believe I am on a beach in South Africa," I say. "This feels like a real summer vacation. Or is it winter vacation?"

Jai laughs. "Either way, we should send a picture to Gemma." Jai pulls out his phone. I hold up my usual peace sign. Jai takes a few photos before saying, "Perfect."

Jai and I find a spot on the beach, and I unfold our beach towels. We're away from the swimmers and the lifeguard station. We didn't come to have fun in the sun. I turn to him.

"So are we starting from scratch or simply reworking?" I ask.

"Can this be saved?" Jai asks. He picks up his guitar, opens the notebook, and begins to sing the latest version of "Run."

Jai has this deep, raspy voice that I've always loved, and it seems perfectly suited to this song. When Jai delivers the last word, I can't help but clap. Though now that he's performed it, I hear how similar the song is to the one Thorn stole. It's clear as day that Jai wrote both of them.

"What if instead of running away, the person is running *to* something?" I ask.

Jai ponders my words. "Not something, but someone."

I nod. And stare down at the finished song. I grab a pen and add "to You" to the title.

"'Run to You,'" Jai says. "I like it. It's romantic."

"This might be the only thing we can use from the old song," I say with a frown. "I think we should rewrite the lyrics."

"We can do this," Jai says. "We're channeling our inner Lorde, remember?"

"Right. You and me. Lorde."

Jai laughs. "Where do we start?"

I study the words, then look up at Jai. I think about how I began liking him, and how it all felt so sudden.

"*It started so suddenly, as I was looking at you*," I say.

"What?" Jai asks.

"The first line of the song can be that. Because love kind of starts suddenly . . ." I trail off.

Jai strums a few chords until he finds a melody he likes. Then he sings the first line. "I like it," he says, smiling.

I write down the lyrics and keep jotting down new ones.

I remember us talking, but you didn't have a clue
My feelings were growing, my longing was showing
I started thinking about you
I started thinking about you

"How's this?" I ask, handing Jai the notebook.

Jai reads them over. "I always knew you were talented, but you hardly ever let me read your songs."

It's true—my songwriting has always been something I've kept to myself. It's a result of my stage fright, I'm sure. But now, with Jai and the band, I'm slowly becoming more confident.

While Jai plays with the melody of the first verse, I take my shoes off and feel the sand between my toes. In the distance, I hear the sound of waves crashing. I write and scratch several lines before I turn my attention to the second verse. I play with different lyrics until I land on something I'm happy with.

You were the sun, and I was the earth
I kept revolving around you
I was the ocean, and you were the shore
I kept breaking for you
There was all this confusion
There was all this emotion

I hold up the notebook to show Jai. I study the lyrics as he plays the guitar. Something doesn't feel quite right yet. I mutter the words over and over again, until finally it dawns on me.

"It should be present tense," I say. "It's not a song about past relationships or heartbreak. It's about the moment you realize you like someone."

"So not a love song," Jai says, "but a crush song?"

How fitting, I think. Of course, I don't tell him any of this. I quickly edit the two verses that we have.

"We still need a chorus and a bridge," I say.

"I don't think we should keep the same structure as 'Run,'" Jai says. "It should be shorter, more poplike, but still very us."

"Run" was written as ABABCB, or verse / chorus / verse / chorus / bridge / chorus.

"So we'll keep the same structure?" I ask.

"Yeah, that should make life easier for us," Jai says.

I edit the first and second verses.

And then I hit a wall. Everything that I come up with after that sucks.

"I think we should take a break," Jai suggests.

I nod. "Yeah, I'm going nowhere with these lyrics."

We pack up our stuff and leave the beach behind. We join the surge of people buzzing down the boardwalk.

Hotels and restaurants tower to the right, and lines of makeshift stalls stretch on our left. Next to us a man sells wire cars. A kid steers their newly bought toy across the sidewalk.

"That's amazing," Jai says.

"I've never seen that before." As Jai and I walk down the sidewalk, we pass stalls selling African art and beadwork. We stop at a kiosk offering handmade beaded jewelry.

"We should get bracelets," I say to Jai. "As a souvenir."

I pick one made of sky-blue beads, and Jai does the same.

"How much is it?" I ask the vendor.

"Twenty rand for two," she says.

I pull out some of the money that Uncle Richard gave us and look down at the different-colored bills with animal faces. I hand over the bronze one with the elephants on the front and Nelson Mandela on the back.

As we leave the stall behind, I can't help but smile at the thought that Jai and I have matching bracelets now. It is something that only we share, and that feels special somehow.

"Let's get some ice cream before heading back to the hotel," I suggest.

We buy two three-scoop vanilla ice creams covered with chocolate sauce and nuts. As we walk back to the Southern Empress, Jai fiddles with his bracelet.

"I guess you'll always have a piece of me with you now," I tease as I hold up my own. And as I do so, the rest of my ice cream lands on the ground. I freeze.

Jai chuckles. "You're just like a kid."

I make an exaggerated pout. "I really wanted that ice cream."

Jai holds out the rest of his. "You can have mine if you want."

Would that be like kissing Jai? It wouldn't. *Calm down, Nate.*

I shake my head. "It's fine." Jai shrugs, unaware of the effect his words have had on me.

Later that afternoon, after a shower and a wardrobe change, we meet Aunt Sylvia and Uncle Richard at Frankie's, a restaurant right on the beach. It has a very laid-back feel to it. Large glass windows show off the amazing ocean view.

"I love this place," Aunt Sylvia says as we take our seats. "They have open mic nights on Saturdays, and that's always a blast."

"Your aunt is known to attempt Whitney Houston songs now and then," Uncle Richard says.

Aunt Sylvia glares at him. "What do you mean, 'attempt'? I totally pull it off."

Jai turns to me. "We should sing something."

I look at him, confused, as if he's grown a second head. "Um, no, thanks. The thought of singing in front of all these people makes me slightly sick."

"This is the next step in overcoming your stage fright," Jai says. "You need to for Ready2Rock. The audience will be much bigger than this. Trust me."

I know that he's right, but I'm not one hundred percent convinced. I guess it doesn't matter, because before I know it, Jai is adding our names to the list of performers. *You can do this, Nate*, I tell myself.

When he returns, I ask, "What song are we singing?"

"Well, you once told me that your dad's favorite song was 'I Don't Want to Miss a Thing' by Aerosmith, so how about that?" Jai suggests.

I only mentioned it in passing, but Jai remembers. This is the first song I learned to play, because I found the sheet music for it in Dad's old guitar case. Emotions swell in my chest.

We watch as people perform, and soon we're called to the stage. It's located at the center of the restaurant, and everyone's looking at us. As we take our places, Jai leans in and whispers in my ear, "I'm right here with you." His breath is warm against the nape of my neck. "I'm not going anywhere."

Jai starts to play the guitar, and I take a deep breath. Even though my heart is hammering away in my chest, I look only at Jai. In my mind, he and I are alone, and I'm singing this song for him.

I begin to perform, and Jai beams at me. With every verse, I get more and more confident, more and more comfortable. Soon my nerves are singing backup and my adrenaline is the lead.

When the music stops, the audience starts clapping, but I'm only looking at Jai. For the first time in my life, I performed in front of strangers, and it's all thanks to him.

<hr />

After dinner Aunt Sylvia suggests we go for a stroll on the beachfront boardwalk. She and Uncle Richard walk ahead of us. As we're walking, fireworks go off.

"Let's go to the pier to see the fireworks," Jai says.

We find a spot along the pier. Reds, blues, and golds explode in loud bangs. We lean against the railing and look up as the night sky becomes living artwork.

I sidle closer to Jai as we watch the loud and colorful display.

Jai and I turn to look at each other. And there's something in his eyes that sets my heart racing. Jai's small smile holds all the things that haven't been said between us yet. I wonder if my smile does the same.

With the spectacle above us and the smell of the ocean in the air, it seems like the perfect moment for a kiss. This is the perfect time for us to cross the line of friendship and step firmly into something more. I want it. And I'm pretty sure Jai wants it too.

He leans in and I do too.

This is it.

The moment I have been waiting for.

Closer.

Almost.

"Nate? Jai?" And just like that, the perfect moment is perfectly ruined. "We lost you for a minute." We pull away just as Aunt Sylvia approaches us. "Enjoying the night view?" she asks.

My heart is still beating in my chest—way too fast. Jai doesn't seem to be faring any better. He's as still as a statue, and I am trying very hard *not* to look at him. If Aunt Sylvia suspects about our almost-lip-lock, she doesn't mention it.

"We should head back to the hotel," she says.

How the hell am I supposed to sleep now when Jai Patel and I almost kissed?

Of course, I don't say any of this.

I just follow her and the boy I almost made out with.

One foot in front of the other.

In my dream I *am* kissing Jai, and it is everything I want it to be and more. It's the scene from last night, except this time we're not interrupted. This time our lips touch. This time we finally confess our feelings for each other.

And then I wake up. It's Jai. But he's not kissing me . . . he's *shaking* me.

I open my eyes with a groan. If it were anyone but Jai, I might have bitten their head off. But the dream is still fresh in my mind, and I can't resist a smile as I look into his eyes.

"Did you have a naughty dream?" Jai asks, bemused.

I flush. "No. Why?" I sound panicked to my own ears.

Jai looks down, and I follow his gaze to a sight that I would like to erase from my memories forever.

"Ah!" I scream, and roll over onto my stomach to hide it. I bury my head under the covers. That's it. This day is canceled. I will not be leaving this bed. Not today. Maybe not ever. This bed will be my final resting place.

Jai laughs and tries to pull the covers from my head, but I hold them tight. I have just embarrassed myself in front of the boy I like by getting a freaking hard-on—tell me what could be worse.

"What were you dreaming of?" Jai teases. "Tell me, tell me, tell me." He's still pulling at the covers. "Or should I be asking, *Who* were you dreaming of?"

Jai pulls on the covers and I let him win. The way he's looking at me, with smoldering eyes, sends a shiver down my spine. Though there's been no physical display of affection between us, it still feels as though we have taken a step forward.

I don't know what we are, but I don't think we're just friends.

"We will never speak of this again," I announce in my most authoritative tone.

Jai, instead of being shaken, laughs. "Wake up," he says after he has calmed down. "We overslept. We're going to be late."

I look at the clock on the bedside table. It's past midday, and our flight back to Jo'burg is at three p.m.

"Shit," I say as I scramble out of bed.

After our almost-kiss last night, Jai and I returned to our hotel room and worked on the song until two in the morning. We edited what we had and completed the rest. With a finished song, I'd say that our Durban songwriting workshop was a success.

We are now officially ready to rock.

20

Ouma Lettie wants us to experience farm life, so all morning Jai and I have been hard at it. Even though I am dirtier and sweatier than I would like to be, I'm happy.

Our morning started with cleaning out the barn of old hay and collecting eggs. This time I braved the coop. But the chickens were nothing compared to the animal that stares me down now: a cow mooing in displeasure.

"You want me to milk *that?*" I ask Ouma Lettie, who's standing behind me.

"I can't let you leave without having you at least try to do it."

"No, thank you," I say. "If that thing sits on me, I will die."

"Don't be so dramatic," Jai says. "I'd love to try it."

"Well, you and the very large cow have fun," I say to him. The cow in question continues to stare at me. She blinks slowly.

"Suit yourself," Ouma Lettie says. She and Jai walk deeper into the cowshed. Jai carries a very large metal pail. I stand my ground, keeping my distance. Farm life is definitely not for me.

I watch as Ouma Lettie guides Jai through the process. She grabs a teat and starts to massage it. Instantly, milk jets out.

"Cool," Jai says. After the demonstration, he sits down next to the cow, who seems unbothered, and takes hold of her teat. Jai squeezes, but nothing happens at first.

I creep toward them, wanting to see the show.

"Don't be afraid to use a bit more force," Ouma Lettie urges.

Jai tries again. And this time milk squirts free.

"You did it," I say.

Jai turns to me, surprised. "When did you come in here?"

"A while ago. You were too udderly distracted to notice," I say, proud of my pun. *Where's my stand-up special, Netflix?*

Jai, however, is completely unappreciative of my comedic chops. "Leave. That was terrible," he says. He continues to milk the cow, and soon his pail is half-full.

"Good job," Ouma Lettie says. She turns to look at me. "Do you want to give it a shot?"

"Still a no," I say. "I can enjoy it as a spectator, but I do *not* want to participate."

"It's not so bad," Jai says. He stands and stretches. The cow moos, and Jai gently rubs her flank. "Good girl."

"I think that's enough farm-life experiences for today," Ouma Lettie says. "You boys go rest up until lunch."

Jai and I decide to explore the farm after polishing off our ham sandwiches. As we leave the house, we spot my archenemy, Thanos. I do not need a repeat of the other day's vicious attack, so I keep my distance from the beastly, angry goose.

We pass the cowshed and see a pen full of goats. We stand

at the wooden fence, and a baby goat looks up and stares at us with curiosity.

"Look at you!" Jai says in a high pitch, but the baby goat scampers away.

"I don't know if I should be offended," I tease. "I've never been rejected so fast in my life."

Jai laughs. "Cute." And I choose to believe that he is referring to me and not the baby goat.

We walk some more, and the fresh farm smell that I've come to enjoy is gone. The air *stinks*. It reeks of waste.

"What is that?" I ask. My nose crinkles from the stench.

"Pigs." Jai points to a pigsty.

The pigs' snorting gets louder and louder. There are six of them in total. The more I look at them, the more I realize they're kind of adorable, especially the piglets.

"I didn't realize how bad a pigsty actually smells," I say as we walk away.

"Yeah, I remember when my parents took my sisters and me to visit a farm. We were supposed to have a picnic, but the terrible smell made us change our plans. It'd taken us over two hours just to get there, and in the end we left without eating." Jai shakes his head. "That was the last time we went out as a family. Before the divorce. Maybe it was a sign."

"Do you still see your dad?" I ask. Jai doesn't really speak much about him.

"Not as often as I used to. He's very busy." Jai smiles. "But he promised to come see us at Ready2Rock."

"Then we'd better win," I say.

"We'll try our best."

"Go, team," I cheer softly.

"Shouldn't it be 'Go, band'?" Jai teases.

I stick my tongue out at him. We exit the first fence of the farm—the one that encloses the yard around the farmhouse. Now we walk on a dirt road past fields and fields of sugarcane—so many. Too many. Once you've seen one, you've kind of seen them all, you know?

Eventually we're too exhausted to keep going, and we stop under a big tree. To our right is another field, this one freshly harvested and bare, and to our left is a large lake. The water glistens in the afternoon sunlight.

"Holy shit, it's hot!" I complain. Sweat trickles down my spine. I am sticky and tired and also more sunburned than I've probably been in my whole damn life. "I think this walk was a bad idea."

Jai laughs. "Yeah, we didn't think this one through." He doesn't seem to have fared any better than me. I turn to him to suggest we go back, and— *Oh, damn.* He's stripped down to his underwear.

"Let's do it," he says. "Let's go swimming."

"The lake has been tempting me since I first saw it," I say.

"If it weren't still light out, I'd totally be losing these too," Jai says, pointing to his underwear. He turns to me, hands on his hips. "Well?"

"Well what?" I ask. I admit that I'm *not* looking at his face. But I can't be blamed.

"Come on, Nate!" Jai says. "Live a little."

I snort. "You're just trying to see me undressed," I tease.

"Busted." Jai laughs. "Seriously, though, let's go swimming."

I look from Jai to the water. It does look super-inviting, and I'm super-hot. "Fine," I say as I peel my shirt off. It's a bit of a struggle considering how sticky I am. After more effort than should be necessary, I kick off my shoes.

"You're going to get your cutoffs wet?" Jai asks. "Don't forget we still have to walk back."

God, considering how far we actually are from the house, Jai makes a damn good point. I unbutton my cutoffs and pull them down. Soon I'm standing in nothing but my checkered boxers. My stomach is flat but with no definition—gym class has always been the bane of my existence.

"Let's do it together." Jai holds out his hand.

I take it. "On three," I say.

"One," we say together. "Two. Three!"

Jai runs full speed toward the water. I try to pull my hand free, but he tightens his grip, saying, "I knew you were going to try that." I am forced to follow him, and we jump into the cold water.

Each movement sends a splash of water against my body. I groan until my body gets used to the temperature, which takes about a minute.

"I didn't expect it to be so cold," I say.

"What are you talking about?" Jai asks. "It's amazing." He's already completely soaked. I, on the other hand, am still splashing my chest to get used to the water.

"Okay, Aquaman," I say.

Jai laughs and sits down in the shallows, close to the bank. He whispers, "This feels so great."

It takes me several tries to sit down too. The lake isn't deep where we are. I don't trust going any farther, at least not without a life jacket. I don't care that Jai is a really good swimmer. Shit happens, and I don't trust deep water.

"I needed this," Jai says as he splashes at me. I return the favor, not foreseeing that this will start a war. Our battle gets more intense, and I stand to get a better advantage. Jai has always been as competitive as I am, which is why I always pick him as my partner for board games. I hate losing, and I make no apology for it.

We run out of the lake, pretend fighting.

"Haven't I already won this game?" Jai teases.

"I don't remember that happening," I reply.

"You're such a sore loser." Jai tackles me and pins my arms down. A minute later, it dawns on us that we are, indeed, semi-undressed. We're skin to skin. Our eyes meet. There's only underwear between our bodies—very, very wet underwear that is clinging to our every nook and cranny.

I feel the sun on my skin, and there's a different kind of fire inside me. Jai lifts his right hand and touches my face. He trails a finger across my jawline to my lips.

Oh, God. This is happening. . . .

This moment has been a long time coming, a dormant volcano waiting to erupt. This is the final line we have to cross to go from friends to something more. My heart is galloping in my chest. I want this. I want him to kiss me.

"Can I?" he asks. His voice is soft.

I nod. And soon his lips are against mine.

My first kiss with Jai Patel is nothing like I've imagined thousands of times before. But it's everything I've ever wanted.

Reality is so much better than whatever I fantasized about. Dreams be damned.

Jai pulls away to take a breath and then kisses me again. I wrap my arms around him and feel the muscles on his back. He rests his forehead against mine. I hear him breathing and feel his heart beating as fast as mine. I never want to leave Jai's arms.

"Wow," he says. "I've wanted to do that for a long time."

"Me too," I say. And then I lean in to kiss him again. Because kissing Jai Patel only twice is not enough. I want more. I *need* more.

I lose track of time—of where my body ends and Jai's begins. I feel as though we're one.

"Now that we've kissed, I kind of don't want to stop," I admit.

"Well, I'm certainly not complaining, but can we get dressed?" Jai asks.

"Yeah, that sounds like a great plan." Our dip in the lake has definitely cooled us down.

We both stand and grab our clothes. Jai lays his T-shirt down under a tree. He sits on it and lies back, then looks at me and pats the ground beside him invitingly.

I follow his lead. Jai pulls me into the crook of his arm. I start to draw patterns on his bare chest. My finger moves toward his pierced nipple. He shivers at the touch, and I chuckle.

"When did you get this?" I ask.

"I got it for my seventeenth birthday," Jai says. He grabs my hand. "You know, you keep touching me and things are happening." We're looking into each other's eyes. He then looks down slowly, and my eyes follow.

Things *sure* have happened.

"Behave," Jai says with an impish grin.

"Fine." I draw out the word. "I'll behave," I say. But I can't stop smiling. Knowing that Jai wants me as much as I want him is a powerful feeling.

It is a feeling I can get used to.

21

Jai and I walk back to the farmhouse hand in hand. We lazed under the tree for the rest of the afternoon. I think I even dozed off for a few minutes.

My phone vibrates—Mom's FaceTiming me. When I answer, her smiling face fills the screen. "Sonno!" she screams, and I watch as Jai disappears into the house.

Mom looks tired. Is she getting enough sleep? And considering that this was meant to be her vacation time, I hate to see her so exhausted.

"Hey, Mom!" I shout back. And I'm just as excited as she is. This is the longest I've ever gone without speaking to her.

"Hold the phone out so I can see you," Mom instructs.

I laugh. "I'm still the same, Mom."

"How's it going?" she asks. The video lags a bit.

"Great! Jai and I are having fun. It's amazing being here. I don't know—it's just peaceful." Had Mom called last week after my encounter with Tommy, this conversation would have taken a very different turn. But after kissing Jai, I'm seeing everything through rose-colored glasses.

"I know the feeling," Mom adds. "When I went there with your dad, I had the best time. Has anyone been mean to you?" Mom asks, and by her tone, I can tell this has been a concern for her. And I'm relieved that I can be honest with her.

"No, everything's fine, Mom. I have Ouma Lettie and Jai. And Meghan and Aunt Sylvia and Uncle Richard. We've been spending a lot of time together. It's been great," I say.

"Oh, yes! I saw some of the photos you posted on Instagram," Mom says. "There's something going on between you and Jai, isn't there?" Teaching Mom how to use social media has been both a blessing and a curse.

"Why are you asking?"

"I saw the way that he was looking at you in that one picture of you guys on the beach. Please tell me, does my son-in-law like you?" Mom has occasionally referred to Jai as her son-in-law. Only in passing and never to his face, so not enough for it to become a massive source of embarrassment. She started calling him this after I said that a pedestrian who looked like Jai was hot. Mom took that little comment and ran with it.

Also, she adores Jai.

"He's not your son-in-law, Mom, but he is kind of maybe going to be my boyfriend." I say those words for the first time. Throughout my relationship with Tommy, I hid things from her. I had to lie about assignments that didn't exist and plans with Gemma that were actually dates with Tommy.

Tommy and I were never boyfriends to anyone but ourselves—and later Gemma. To everyone else, we were always just friends. Buddies. And when people got curious about us, we would always have a story. A cover.

With Jai there is no lie. There is no story. It's all in the open, I guess. I like Jai and I want to date him. I want him to be my boyfriend. And, God, it feels good to say.

Mom screams—louder and longer than before. Oh, our fusspot, Mr. Schuster, is definitely on his way down now with a complaint. "Oh my God, oh my God, oh my God. Tell me everything!" Mom says.

She seems more excited than I am—which is almost impossible, to be honest. I still can't believe that I kissed Jai. And I want to keep doing it.

"There isn't much to tell, really. We both just like each other," I say.

"For how long?" Mom asks.

"A while now," I admit.

"Why didn't you tell me?" she asks.

"Mom, please. I'd like to keep some things to myself," I say. "Also, enough with the twenty questions, Mom."

"Fine," she says. "I'll stop. But you're going to tell me everything when you get back next weekend."

"Sure thing," I say. I will tell her a heavily edited version of our story—how edited it will need to be is yet to be determined.

Mom brings a hand to her mouth in an over-the-top fake cry. "I can't believe my baby boy has a boyfriend. His first boyfriend."

I don't have the heart to break it to her, and maybe I never will tell her about Tommy.

"Stop being so dramatic," I say. "And you wonder why I'm the way I am?"

"You are perfect," Mom says. "From head to toe. From the inside out. Perfection." Mom does a chef's kiss.

I laugh. "I miss you."

"I miss you too," Mom says. Then a moment later she shouts toward the door: "Coming!"

"Is it Mr. Schuster?" I ask.

Mom rolls her eyes. "I've never wanted to beat a man so much in my life."

"Violence is not the answer. Please. Try to stay calm," I warn.

"We'll see how he behaves today," Mom says. "Anyway, let me go deal with him. Oh, and tell my son-in-law I say hello."

"Fine, I will," I say. "Try to ignore whatever Mr. Schuster says."

"I'll try. No promises, though." Mom kisses the phone goodbye. "Love you, Sonno!"

"Love you more," I say, and hang up.

With a smile plastered on my face, I head inside the house and find Jai talking with Ouma Lettie. Whatever he's said made her laugh. Jai's changed out of his wet clothes, and his hair is tied in a loose ponytail. He looks so good. It's no wonder I'm falling for him as hard as I am.

He must feel the weight of my eyes, because he turns around and catches me staring.

"Do I have something on my face?"

"No, I just like looking at you," I tease.

"Staring will cost you." And with that Jai leans in and gives me a quick peck on the cheek. "Paid in full."

Ouma Lettie made vetkoeks for dinner. Vetkoek is a traditional South African fried bread dough. We eat them with a mince curry. They're so good, I go for seconds.

After dinner, I'm in my room reading when it starts to storm—loudly and angrily. I jump off the bed and watch as the rain hits against the window. Lightning flashes in the distance, and a few heartbeats later thunder rumbles.

"I was going to ask if you wanted to practice the song," Jai says from behind me. I turn to find him leaning against the door and holding his guitar. "But the storm is too loud."

"It must be because the house is old. It seems louder somehow," I say, and throw myself on the bed.

Jai comes in and sits down on the floor. He starts to plug away at some chords. He finds the perfect melody to accompany the storm.

"I told my mom about us," I say after a while.

Jai stops playing and turns to me. "What did you say?"

"Just that we might soon start dating?" I look at him. "We will start dating, right?"

Jai chuckles. "That's the plan," he says. "I mean, I've liked you for a long time."

This is shocking. I spent so long thinking my feelings were one-sided.

"What are you talking about? When did it start for you?" I ask. "Liking me, I mean?"

I'm startled by how fast Jai answers the question.

"The moment I saw you playing my song on the piano."

I sit up. "The day we met?"

I remember. It was mid-October, and Gemma had one of her many club meetings during lunch. So I was alone in the music room. I technically wasn't allowed to be in there, but no one really checked, and when they did, Ms. Franklin, the music teacher, always covered for me.

I'd been twiddling with a few keys on the piano, and soon an easy melody filled the space. It wasn't long before the tune morphed into something with intent and thought. The melody of "Antihero" started, and as my fingers danced across the black and white keys, I began to sing. My version of the song was much slower than the original, turning an up-tempo rock song into a ballad.

"Antihero" was a song I'd stumbled across by accident. It was by an indie band known as Infinite Sorrow. I didn't know much else about the song, or about the band for that matter, but it was slowly becoming one of my favorites.

It was an anthem to my heartbreak. Tommy Herron had already ghosted me by then, leaving me nothing more than a brokenhearted boy. With my eyes closed, I reached the crescendo and hit the high note in the song's second chorus. I ended the song strong, delivering the last of the lyrics twenty seconds before the end of the song. The rest was all piano.

My fingers stilled, and the sound of clapping startled me. My eyes shot open and found Jai Patel standing at the door.

At the time, Jai was just the aloof new kid with ripped black jeans and a leather jacket that had seen better days. He was something different in a town that was mostly all the same. Everyone knew everyone, that sort of thing. But Jai, he was a mystery. And so he was on everyone's lips . . . everyone's but mine, that is.

"Not bad, Nate," Jai said. "How do you know that song?"

"What are you doing here?" I asked. This place was off-limits to students.

"It's rude to answer a question with a question," he said with a smirk.

I remember being annoyed and making a move to exit the music room, but Jai stopped me by putting an arm across the doorway. This was the closest I'd ever been to him. At the time, it was the most we'd ever actually spoken to each other.

"Tell me how you know that song," Jai demanded again.

"Why does it matter?" I snapped. "Can you move?" Jai didn't budge. I sighed. "It's just a song I like."

Surprise fluttered across his face. "You like *my* song?"

"Your song? What are you talking about? It's by a band called Infinite Sorrow."

"I know," Jai said. "That's my band." After dropping this bombshell, Jai spun on his heel. He paused to say, "See you around, Nate."

And that was how Jai and I met—officially. If I'm honest, I think that was also the time I started to be intrigued by him.

I leave behind the memory.

"Why didn't you tell me sooner?" I ask.

Jai shrugs. "It didn't feel like the right time," he says. "Besides, I was also scared of ruining our friendship. I don't know. Being here in South Africa with you has made me braver. I've found the courage to say that I want to date you, Nate."

"So we're dating, then?" I ask. "You're officially my boyfriend."

"Official. *Official.*" Jai smiles. "I want to tell everyone that you're my boyfriend. Shout it from the rooftops. Jai and Nate are dating!"

I laugh and watch as Jai stands. He puts his guitar down.

"What are you doing?" I ask.

"You need to return the favor," Jai says.

"What favor?" Jai jumps onto the bed, and I make room for him. He turns to me and lies in the crook of my arm.

"This favor," he says.

"You sure you want to be this close?" I ask. "Thunderstorms can be very romantic."

Jai laughs. "All the more reason to." He kisses my cheek. "I can't believe I get to do that now."

"If you want to kiss me, kiss me properly," I tease.

"Is that a challenge?" Jai says. He rises up on one elbow before I can even say anything. Jai's face hovers above mine.

"Kiss me, Jai Patel," I say. And he does. Our lips meet, and a lock of Jai's hair dances against my cheek. Our breathing gets heavier. His lips travel down the side of my neck and I shiver. I grab ahold of his face and bring him back to my lips. I reach to unbutton his shirt.

Both our chests are thumping now. I ask, "Are you okay with this?"

"Yes," Jai says. He's straddling me now. He pulls off his shirt and pauses. "Are you?"

"More than okay with it." I run my hand down the expanse of his body—from the chest down, down, *down.*

Jai shivers at my touch. We both lose the rest of our clothes faster than I would've thought possible. When we're only in our underwear, I kiss Jai once more. It's deep and weighted by desire. I bite on his lip.

I study him. He is beautiful. Sexy. Perfect.

This won't be my first time. And I know from previous conversations with Jai that he isn't a virgin either. I stand up.

"Do you want to stop?" Jai asks, his voice rough.

"No, it's not that," I say. I run to my luggage and start looking. Even though I was so embarrassed and against the very thought of having these condoms, I have to thank Meghan. I guess she read me and Jai right.

I hold up the strip. Jai reaches out to me. He nuzzles into my neck once more. "You've come prepared."

Thank you, Meghan!

Jai and I use them—as in, more than one.

22

My *boyfriend* Jai Patel decided not to come on this tour with me. Honestly, I don't think I'll ever get tired of saying that. He's back at the farm resting for the big party tonight—or banquet, as it is being referred to on the itinerary.

Aunt Sylvia offered to send a driver when I texted her that I wanted to go on the historical tour today. So I'm in the car on my way to a township called Soweto. Apparently it was created during the apartheid regime for Black people to live in.

When I arrive at Vilakazi Street, I'm startled to find Tommy sitting on a bench waiting. For a moment I debate whether I should get out of the car, but in the end I decide that I need to stop letting Tommy have such a hold over me. I've moved on.

I can do this.

I thank the driver, get out of the car, and walk to the ticket office to get my tour pass. It's then that Tommy notices me. He looks shocked to see me too, before his face becomes an unreadable mask. In the past I could always read him, like a beloved book, but our time apart has changed that.

"Hey, Nate," he says after I've received my ticket and checked in for the morning tour of Soweto.

"Hey." I can be civil and polite. I can rise above it all. I have a boyfriend now, and I am more than happy, and nothing that Tommy Herron does will bring me down.

"You came alone?" he asks, scanning the crowd of strangers behind me.

"Yeah, I'm the only history buff," I say. I search for more wedding guests but find none. Which is very surprising. Maybe everyone is busy getting ready for the party tonight.

"Me too," Tommy says. And he smiles that old smile of his, the one that used to make my heart race and flutter.

Tommy and I always had things in common, our love of history being one of them. We liked the same movies and music, so our dates were always fun because we were both doing things we enjoyed. Our relationship worked really well—until it didn't, of course.

Once everyone has checked in, we begin the tour. A middle-aged woman steps to the center of the crowd of fourteen or so people. "Hello, everyone. It's wonderful to have you all here. My name is Thembi, and I will be your guide. The tour centers on Vilakazi Street in Soweto," Thembi explains. "It is the only street in the world to have been home to two Nobel laureates: the late former president of South Africa and the first democratically elected one, Nelson Mandela; and Archbishop Emeritus Desmond Tutu. Actually, Tutu still lives here with his wife and can even be seen strolling the streets from time to time.

"There will be three main stops on this tour today," Thembi continues. "First, we will visit the Mandela House museum, which is of course the former president's house. After, we will make our way to the Hector Pieterson Memorial and Museum before finally ending the tour with a trip to the Apartheid Museum. If there are no questions, let's begin, shall we?"

We follow Thembi as she leads us to our first stop. Tommy falls into step beside me, and I hate to admit how natural it feels. Even though we haven't seen each other in so long, I am used to having him around. Granted, what we've been through has tainted and changed what I feel about him, but he'll never be a stranger.

"I can't believe we get to learn about apartheid in South Africa. How wild is that?" Tommy asks. And he sounds so moved by it. I have to admit I am too. It's why I came on this tour even though Jai opted out. As someone with an interest in history, I couldn't pass on the chance to participate. Knowing that experiences like this don't come often, I decide to lower my defenses toward Tommy. Let bygones be bygones, if just for today.

For this tour we can be friendly, or friendly-adjacent—whatever that is.

We come to a stop outside our first destination. Thembi turns to us and points at the humble redbrick house in front of us. A wall has 8115 VILAKAZI STREET, ORLANDO WEST, SOWETO written on it, and beside it stands a glass panel that reads MANDELA HOUSE.

"The house was built in 1945, and you can still see scorch marks from petrol bombs and bullet holes in the walls from when Nelson Mandela was in prison for twenty-seven years."

As we start to move through the house, Tommy pulls out a camera and begins to snap photos. I take out my cell phone and do the same.

On one of the shelves sits a pair of old boots worn by Nelson Mandela himself. A wall holds all the honorary doctorates that he had bestowed upon him by universities and institutions around the world. Standing in the center of the room, I can't fathom what this man must have been through. This was his home, a place he was not allowed to see for twenty-seven years while he served his prison sentence.

"Do you want me to take a photo of you?" Tommy asks. He holds out his hand for my phone. I do want pics to show Mom.

"Thanks," I say.

"You're welcome," Tommy says as he takes a few photos of me.

"These four walls were where Tata, which means 'Father,' laid his head. Where his wife, the late Winnie Madikizela-Mandela, raised their two daughters," Thembi says. "This was the home of the great man who helped South Africa become the country that it is today. To this day we thank him. May he forever rest in peace. Amandla. Which means 'power' or 'strength.'"

Our next stop is the Hector Pieterson Memorial and Museum. I learned about Nelson Mandela in history, but Hector Pieterson is new to me, and I'm thankful to have Thembi with us.

"Hector Pieterson was one of the children who died in the Soweto Uprising on June sixteenth, 1976. The Black schoolchildren protested being forced to learn in Afrikaans in township schools—many of them did not know the language at all. While the youth started to sing the banned liberation anthem 'Nkosi Sikelel' iAfrika'—'Lord Bless Africa'—the police opened fire. About twenty children were murdered." Thembi points at a large picture. "This photo of a dying Hector Pieterson being carried by a student while his sister runs beside them has become synonymous with the Soweto Uprising." Thembi turns to us. "June sixteenth is now honored as Youth Day. We acknowledge the bravery and sacrifice of these youths who looked racism in the eye and fought back."

Tommy and I explore the museum, which is filled with other photos of that day. As we're walking, Tommy grabs me by the arm to stop me from colliding with someone. I've been so focused on the exhibit that I haven't been paying attention.

"Careful," Tommy warns.

"Sorry, and thanks," I say. "I think I'm too invested in the stuff we don't get to learn about in history back home."

"I know what you mean," Tommy agrees.

"There's so much that's left out of the textbooks—not just world history but some of our own American history too," I say.

Tommy and I come to a stop in front of a photograph of a group of teenagers. To think they were my age, children who stood against hate. Hector Pieterson was an innocent child when the apartheid police killed him. It's sad to think that stuff like this is still happening in the world today—the police, instead of protecting us, are still killing us.

The final stop on the tour is the Apartheid Museum. We all climb into a minibus, which they call a taxi here, and make the twenty-minute trip to our destination. Before we enter the museum, we're each given a ticket at random. Some say BLANKES / WHITES and others say NIE-BLANKES / NON-WHITES, and each ticket leads us through a separate entrance. This is how it was back then: a country divided between white and nonwhite. I put my ticket in my pocket to save as a memento. Once inside the museum, we rejoin our tour guide.

The museum has twenty-two exhibition areas that detail the rise and fall of the apartheid regime, the dark past of South Africa.

"Starting in 1948, the white elected National Party started a process that would make millions of people second-class citizens," Thembi explains. "The most affected were Black South Africans, but coloreds and Indians were also treated as beneath white people. They also couldn't enter 'whites only' spaces and had specific areas where they were allowed to live.

"Apartheid lasted until 1994, when Nelson Mandela was elected president. During that period, racism became the law of the land, and those regarded as 'less than' were put through years of servitude, humiliation, and abuse. This museum was created to share the darkest days of South Africa but also some of its greatest triumphs."

Thembi leads us into the first exhibit room. "Within the halls of this museum a story will unfold, one detailing the state-sanctioned system based solely on racism. You will be angry, you will be sad, but it is our wish that you will walk away with a deeper understanding and appreciation for this country and all it has been through."

After her introduction, Thembi leaves us to experience the museum on our own, at our own pace. Tommy and I walk through the halls, turning left into a room with a gate like a jail cell. A collection of nooses dangles overhead, and a photo on the wall shows how they were used during apartheid for political executions.

Another room has the signposts that were prevalent during the time: WHITES ONLY in big, bold lettering. Every sign where I see those racist words makes me angry. As do the enlarged passbooks that hang on the wall. Every Black person aged sixteen or older had to carry a dompas, a document that showed where they could live and work.

To think some monster thought up this regime and made countless people suffer for it. The more I see, the closer to tears I get.

"Are you okay?" Tommy asks. His voice is soft and kind. He rests a hand on my shoulder, and I let him.

"I guess this all hits close to home because it affected members of my family," I say. "My dad grew up in this time; my dad—who would still be alive if it weren't for the accident—lived through this. That's how recent it is."

Tommy shakes his head. "I guess reading about it in a textbook makes it seem long-ago, but it hasn't been that long at all." He squeezes my shoulder and lets go.

"You're right," I say.

Tommy always was a good listener.

We walk on. Tommy and I spend the rest of the time wandering from exhibit to exhibit. And it's comfortable. With a start, I realize that I don't altogether hate spending time with him.

It isn't like it was before, and that's okay, because I don't need it to be. What we were is over, but this isn't all that bad.

Maybe this is the first step to closure.

23

After the tour ends, the driver picks me up on Vilakazi Street and drives me to Sandton—the business hub of Johannesburg. It's where I'm set to meet Meghan and Jai. For what, exactly? I'm not sure, but Meghan has been adamant about meeting us there.

When I arrive at the rendezvous point—a large, bustling mall made of brick and glass—I find Jai and Meghan waiting outside.

"What are we doing here?" I ask.

"We're grabbing lunch!" Meghan explains. "We'll get our hair done and get you some suits afterward, but we need fuel first."

I don't argue the point, because I'm hungry too. We follow as Meghan leads us into the shopping center. Soon we arrive at a place called King Curries. "Since you're in South Africa, you have to taste a bunny chow."

"Bunny chow?" I ask. "Like rabbits?"

Meghan laughs. "No, it's not made with rabbits. How hot do you like your food?"

"I'm not good with hot food," I admit.

Meghan turns to Jai. "And you?"

"I'll have the hot one," Jai says.

Meghan nods and turns her attention to the counter attendant. "We'll take three mutton bunnies, one mild and two hot, please."

Jai and I grab seats while Meghan pays for the food. I choose the chair next to a window, and Jai sits beside me. We're both wearing shorts, and I feel our knees touching. Feeling his skin against mine, I flash back to last night—a night I will remember for the rest of my life. I still can't believe this boy beside me is my boyfriend.

"I played some of 'Run to You' for Raquel, and she loved it," Jai says. "Apparently it's a very accurate description of what having a crush on someone is like."

"Well, we would have experience with that, wouldn't we?" We look at each other and smile.

"Can you two stop making such lovey-dovey eyes at each other?" Meghan says when she joins us. "I'm going to get jealous."

"You are literally getting married at the end of the week. Why would you be jealous?" I ask.

"I too want to be young and in love." Meghan sighs wistfully.

"Again, I repeat: You are getting married. Is that not the epitome of 'young and in love'?"

"Getting married is a lot of pressure, okay?" Meghan whines. "Let me be a romantic at heart."

Jai chuckles. "Stop stressing out the bride-to-be, Nate."

"Yes, Nate. Stop stressing me out," Meghan echoes.

I dramatically zip my lips shut.

Fifteen minutes later a server comes over with our bunny chows. The bunny chow turns out to be a loaf of bread quartered and filled with mutton curry. It's served with a side of carrot salad.

I watch Meghan use her hands to eat it. Soon Jai follows suit, and I join in too. The food is delicious, and even though mine is "mild," I still sniff throughout the meal. Meghan does too.

"I always say if your nose doesn't run while eating curry, then it isn't curry." Meghan takes a sip of her Coke. "So how was it? A taste unique to South Africa."

"Great," Jai says. He licks his thumb. *Why do I find this hot?* "It's definitely something I could eat again."

Full from lunch, we leave the shopping center and pile into Meghan's car. I notice she's driving a different one today. I want to ask her whether she has a car for every day of the week, but I decide not to, because the answer might depress me. I've been working at Big Mo's to save up for just *one* car to use during college.

The car we're in is a silver Jeep, meaning that Jai will not need to become human origami in the back seat. Meghan pulls out of the parking lot and joins traffic.

We arrive at the salon ten minutes and a bumpy car ride later. My hair is trimmed and styled. Of the three of us, I'm done first. I watch as Jai gets his blow-dried and styled in a topknot. This style on him is becoming a favorite of mine.

Meghan, on the other hand, has a crown of very large rollers. And as they are removed, her locks form waves and waves of perfect curls. Kept in place by spray and skill, Meghan's hair is beautiful.

We pile back into Meghan's Jeep and drive off to a boutique. It's located on the first floor of a skyscraper. Meghan stops the car, and a valet comes to park it for her.

"Welcome, Ms. Hargreaves," an employee says when we enter the store, and Meghan wiggles her fingers in a wave. "We've reserved suite A for you and your party."

Everything about this place screams expensive. Dark hardwood floors are polished to perfection, French love seats and armchairs have been carefully positioned for customers to sit, soft classical music wafts from hidden speakers, and a large gold-and-crystal chandelier hangs above us.

I lean in toward Meghan and whisper in her ear, "Jai and I don't really need clothes."

"Nonsense. You do. A lot of fancy people are attending tonight. Besides, it isn't only you."

"What do you mean?" I ask.

"Mom and I dressed my other American friends too. And they're getting their hair and makeup done back at the house. Consider it a perk of being a guest for the wedding."

"Still—" I start to argue, but Meghan hushes me.

"You can wear this suit again, to the wedding. It's an investment. Now, please, let's get started. Time's a-wasting, and I can't be late to my own party, ya know."

I stop myself from snorting. Meghan believes in being fashionably late to everything, so that's a bald-faced lie. Even so, I let her get away with it. I allow myself to be swept up in the makeover process.

Jai and I try on suit after suit, waiting for Meghan's approval. I get it first. The suit she deems best for me looks almost like a normal tuxedo, except for the white hand-painted flower branches up the legs of the trousers and the sides of the jacket.

Jai steps out from behind the changing curtain, and instantly I know this is the one. Meghan agrees, because we both say "Damn" in unison.

Jai's suit is a sleek, three-piece black-and-white pinstripe. It also has red roses painted on it.

"You really cannot go wrong with McQueen," Meghan says. "Simply perfection."

McQueen is a name I've only heard on TV, and yet here we are, wearing designer clothes. I don't look at the price tag because it's in rand anyway.

"Go stand next to Jai," Meghan tells me. "I want to take a picture for your mom." Meghan turns to the employee who's been assisting us. "We'll take the Alexander McQueen and the Haider Ackermann, thanks."

I catch sight of Jai and me in the mirror. We look good.

"I think we have our prom outfits," Jai whispers to me.

"Are you asking me to prom?" I ask. Prom is almost a year away, but Jai clearly has long-term plans for us. My heart swells in my chest.

"Yes, Nate. Will you be my plus-one?"

I laugh. "So this is an ongoing theme now?"

"Is that a yes?" Jai asks, smiling.

I lean against his shoulder. "Of course. It's a date."

24

I've never attended a banquet before, and so as we're driven up the driveway, I'm a mix of nerves and excitement. This is the first time that I will be seeing a lot of my extended family this week. And I feel a little nervous.

I only hope I survive this relatively unscathed.

"You'll be fine," Jai assures me. After the boutique, Meghan dropped us off at the farm, and now we're in the back seat of yet another car owned by her family. Jai takes my hand in his. At moments like this, it feels like it's always been meant to be. "You have me."

"You've been flirting with me nonstop lately," I tease, and squeeze his hand.

"I'm just making up for lost time," Jai says.

"Careful, or it might get you into trouble," I continue to tease.

Jai smirks. "I wouldn't mind. Especially with you."

And it feels like we are on the precipice of misbehaving. If we don't stop now, we may start doing some *things* that are not appropriate to be done in a back seat—at least while there's a driver present.

When the car stops, we get out and are greeted by the warm evening air. A large fountain illuminated by a flood of lights is behind us. All around us, guests get out of their modes of transportation and make their way to the venue's entrance.

The banquet is being hosted in a mansion, which looks like several cubes stacked against and on top of one another. Some are made of concrete and others of glass. The building, which probably cost a ton of money and was designed by a world-class architect, belongs in *Architectural Digest*.

The sounds of chatter and music fill the air in the foyer. I almost can't believe that I am invited to *this* party. This is the lifestyle of the damn filthy rich. It's the stuff you see on Instagram and think *If only*. All around me are people wearing very expensive clothes. I look down at my own. Tonight I'm one of them. I can be a part of the fantasy.

We've arrived here just in time, because we see Aunt Sylvia and Uncle Richard approach the foot of the staircase. Uncle Richard is in a classic tuxedo, and Aunt Sylvia is wearing an emerald gown that is undoubtedly by some famous designer.

Aunt Sylvia motions for Meghan and Ben to join them. The couple looks picture-perfect, and when they gaze at each other, it's clear as day they're very much in love.

Aunt Sylvia holds up a flute of champagne. The crowd begins to hush, and she waits a moment before speaking. "Thank you all for coming. I'm glad you could join us on such a joyous occasion. We're very happy to be adding a wonderful member to our family. Meghan and Ben have been friends for years, and I am overjoyed that they fell in love with each other. They are perfectly suited for one another. Please, everyone, let's toast and celebrate the couple."

The crowd cheers, and those with drinks take a sip. Soon the music starts again, and the guests begin to socialize like before. After the toast, Meghan comes floating toward us. She's wearing a dress by some *V* designer—Valentino or Versace or something. The dress is red and has two layers of fabric. The one beneath is solid and a deeper red than the outer one, which is sheer. It's a long-sleeved gown with a collar, and it has flower embroidery on it. Meghan looks beautiful, and if this is what she's wearing tonight, I can only imagine what her wedding dress will be like.

"You boys can have some champagne, you know," Meghan says. "Wait, how old are you?"

"You don't know when my birthday is?" I ask.

"Of course I know," Meghan says with a shake of her head, clearly meaning no. "But seriously, are you both eighteen?"

"Seventeen," Jai and I say in unison. Jai and I are both Aquarians.

Meghan ponders this for a moment before saying, "Close enough. We'll just round up for tonight and say you're eighteen."

Meghan grabs two flutes of champagne from a server. "You know what they say—when in Rome, do as the Romans do." She hands us the glasses.

Jai and I share a glance before accepting the drinks. It isn't the first time I've tasted alcohol, but it sure is the first time I'm drinking champagne—and the expensive stuff at that. I take a sip and smack my lips at the taste.

"Huh, so this is what money tastes like," I say.

Jai takes a sip too. "Wow. That's good."

Meghan smiles. "Now, please, let's not overdo it. Drink responsibly and all that." She gets pulled away by another guest.

I turn to Jai. "Do you want to check out the rest of the house with me?"

"Yes," Jai says. "I want to take a few pictures too."

As we walk deeper into the mansion, I ask, "Can you believe that there are people who live like this?"

"They're your family, Nate," Jai says.

"That may be true, but we live in very different worlds. I mean, look at this living room. It's the size of our whole apartment." I point at the leather couch with chrome finishes that looks way too low and hard to be comfortable. "I bet you it costs as much as my apartment."

The living room is white with black accents. There's a glass door that acts as one of the walls, and it's been folded to allow guests in and out of the space. To my right is an exposed-brick wall with a fireplace.

The kitchen is a modern masterpiece, and in the dining room a buffet table stretches under a large chandelier.

"Let's go upstairs," I say to Jai.

After some exploring, Jai and I end up on a balcony. Jai leans in and kisses me, a peck at first, but I deepen it. We pull back smiling.

"I've wanted to do that all night," Jai says.

"Me too."

We lean against a glass railing and look down at the guests who are hanging out below us.

"You know, I've only ever seen houses like this when my sister was watching HGTV," Jai says.

This house really does feel unreal.

With our minitour complete, Jai and I head back inside. We return to the food table. I'm eating a samosa when suddenly I feel the weight of someone's eyes on me. It's Tommy.

After this morning, the sight of Tommy doesn't make me recoil. Jai must notice, because he says, "You're not scowling. Why aren't you scowling?"

"He was on the tour with me this morning," I say. I meant to tell Jai about it right away, but the afternoon was jam-packed and I forgot. But Jai doesn't seem to mind.

"Did you guys finally talk?" he asks.

"Not about anything important," I say.

25

I'm desperately looking for a bathroom when I hear someone call my name. I recognize Tommy's voice before I turn around.

We haven't argued today, but that doesn't mean that I want to go out of my way to spend time with him. Besides, I really, really need to go. Still, I send a mental apology to him.

Sorry, Tommy, no time right now.

I sprint up the stairs two at a time and turn into the first room I see. Hopefully, there's a bathroom here. This guest room makes my room back home look like a shoe closet.

In a house like this, I assume that each room has a bathroom, and I'm relieved to see this is true. I pee and wash my hands. My reflection in the mirror catches my eye. *Looking good, Nate.* Clothes really do make a world of difference.

Before going back downstairs, I go out on the balcony.

"Nathan." I hear a voice behind me. Uncle Richard is leaning against the balcony door, lighting a cigarette. "I've been looking for you."

I haven't had a chance to speak to him or Aunt Sylvia tonight.

Uncle Richard pats me on my back—harder than is really necessary, if I'm being honest. I brush it off with a smile. "I keep forgetting how tall you've grown." He squints at me, studying me. "You're probably as tall as your dad was." He takes a pull of his cigarette before exhaling a cloud of smoke. He sees me watching him smoke and misunderstands. Uncle Richard holds out the cigarette, but I shake my head.

"No, thanks," I say. "I don't smoke."

Uncle Richard shrugs. "Fair enough." He takes a drag of his cigarette and exhales. "It's best you don't get started," he says. "Your dad never did."

"Yeah, my mom hates smoking," I say. Mom lost her mother to lung cancer. Mom says Grandma was practically a walking chimney.

"Your mother hates smoking, but she doesn't hate you being a *moffie*?" Uncle Richard shakes his head. I notice too late that something seems different about Uncle Richard. The way he's looking at me now isn't like before. It feels colder. Now that we're alone, something has changed.

"Moffie?" I ask. I've never heard the word before. It sounds strange in my mouth.

"Gay," Uncle Richard says with a condescending sneer. I don't have to Google this word to know it's a slur. Uncle Richard wants to hurt me—and he is.

Uncle Richard studies me. "Your mom has done a mostly fine job with you. But I suppose this is why you need a man in your life when you're young," he says. "It's a pity your dad died when he did."

"What do you mean?" I ask. I *know* what he's insinuating. But I want him to say it. I want him to say the words, even if they cause me pain.

"I doubt you'd have turned out the way you are if he were still around," Uncle Richard says. "I was happy to meet Jai because I thought he would be a good manly influence on you, help you outgrow this phase of yours. But I saw you two kissing. I was clearly wrong."

I open my mouth to say something—*anything*—but the words die at my lips. I was not prepared for this. My fear and anxiety vanished after the cookout with Uncle Richard. He was treating me as usual. I didn't think that would change, and so suddenly.

Whether Dad was alive or not, I'd still be gay. I want to tell Uncle Richard that, but I can't. Sometimes you imagine exactly what you would say and do in a situation, but when you find yourself in it, you just stand still.

I am a deer in the headlights.

I'm struggling to breathe under the weight of Uncle Richard's judgment and disappointment. This man is like a stranger, not at all like the uncle I spent time with during this trip.

"There you are!" Jai says. Relief floods through my body. I'm pretty sure my shoulders relax. He comes to stand next to me while Uncle Richard studies him. My uncle's eyes aren't friendly—not anymore—but Jai chooses to overlook the hostility. Instead, he smiles.

"It's good to see you again, sir," Jai says. He holds out his hand to shake Uncle Richard's. Uncle Richard ignores it.

"We should go," I whisper to Jai.

Jai nods. He interlocks his fingers with mine. We don't say anything else as Jai leads me from the balcony. As we walk, I can feel Uncle Richard's eyes burning a hole through my back.

"I'm sorry," I say when we get inside.

I replay Uncle Richard's words over and over in my head.

"I wasn't going to eavesdrop and intervene, but he said some stuff that was pretty messed up," Jai says. "His homophobic bullshit is not your fault."

"You heard that?" I ask.

Jai nods. "You were gone for so long that I wanted to check on you."

"Thank you," I say. "For getting me out of there."

"I wanted us to get together on this trip, but being your shield was part of the gig."

"But who shields you?" I ask.

"I'm fine," Jai says. "It's like water off a duck's back."

"I wish it was like that for me."

"I get it. It hurts more because it's so close to home." Jai shakes his head and sighs bitterly. "It's always more painful when it's family."

I shake my head. "I don't know where it came from. He's known I'm gay this whole time. What changed? I just don't understand."

Jai squeezes the hand that he is still holding.

"I'm tired," I tell him. "I think I've had enough." Uncle Richard was my clock hitting midnight. I'm done.

Jai nods. "Let's go find our driver."

Jai is still holding my hand when we walk down the stairs.

A few people stare, but we ignore them. We see Tommy as we pass the kitchen. Jai and I run out of the foyer. We find our driver and head back to the farm.

On the way home, I close my eyes. Jai is still holding my hand.

I just want to forget that tonight ever happened.

26

I toss and turn all night. I wake up and run a hand through my hair, pulling it in frustration. I keep hearing Uncle Richard's words. His slur.

Thank God for Jai Patel.

He helped me tonight. My knight in designer armor. Jai. Jai. Jai. The more I think about him, the harder I seem to be falling for him. I'd hate for any of our blissful and beautiful moments on this trip to be tainted by last night.

Last night with Jai was everything. I was enjoying time with my boyfriend. It's upsetting that we even have to think about being affectionate in public—being happy. Just because we're gay doesn't mean we can't be any of those things. That people like Uncle Richard want to make it seem so is messed up. There is no "different." There is no "normal." There are only people—and our happiness, at the end of the day, is all that matters.

I look at my phone—five a.m. I walk downstairs in need of a distraction. I silently move about the house, but I'm startled to find that some of the lights downstairs are on. I pause and listen. There are sounds coming from the porch swing.

I make my way over to find Ouma Lettie there with a cup of tea and Roscoe and Coco at her feet. She turns to me.

"Shouldn't you still be sleeping?" she asks.

"I can't. Too much on my mind." Ouma Lettie nods her understanding. "Why are you awake so early?" I ask.

"When you get to my age, sleep comes and goes. Lying in bed aimlessly just makes my bones ache. So I'd rather watch the sun rise."

Seeing a sunrise seems like a better use of my time than suffering while trying to sleep, so I join Ouma Lettie. For a while we sit in silence, until finally she breaks it.

"So how was it last night?" she asks. "Did you have fun?"

"It was . . . different," I say. "I guess I'm not used to the glitz and the glamour."

Ouma Lettie laughs. "I'm the same. It's so foreign to me. And at my age I don't have the energy for such things.

"You and Jai looked wonderful," she adds.

She was asleep when we came home, so how did she see us?

Ouma Lettie explains before I ask. "Meghan sent me a photo of you two. You looked happy."

"I am happy," I say. And for the most part it's true. But stuff like last night can be a real damper. "Do you think Dad would have been okay with me?"

I don't know what makes me ask. I think it's a question that has been locked in my heart for a very long time. It is something I've always wondered. Whether he would have been as accepting as Mom. And now, on the heels of Uncle Richard's remarks, I wonder if Dad would've felt the same way as his brother.

"Your father would be so proud of you," Ouma Lettie says. "He would've loved you and whomever you love."

"Are you okay with it?" I ask. "That I'm gay?"

Ouma Lettie pauses. "I can say that without a doubt I support and love you. It doesn't matter to me whom you love. Given my life, I'd be a hypocrite to think otherwise. I spent it all fighting for my own right to love in a way that society deemed 'different' and 'inappropriate.'" She turns to look at me. "I was a white woman daring to love a man of color during apartheid. And just like I felt then, I feel now. Whoever thinks that they have a right to tell you who to be and whom to love can simply be ignored—and that includes your uncle Richard."

My heart swells at the certainty that I've always had another warrior by my side. Ouma Lettie loves and supports me, and that's enough. Just like she said, everyone else doesn't matter.

"Uncle Richard really hurt me last night," I say.

"I won't make excuses for his behavior, but I will apologize for the hurt he caused you." Ouma Lettie rests her wrinkled and callused hand on mine. "I want you to be happy, Nathan. And you need to live in the way that makes you happy." Ouma Lettie smiles. "If I had listened to the people around me, my own family, I would never have been happy. I don't regret loving your grandfather one bit. I would make the same choices again and again, because with your grandfather I was my happiest."

She sighs.

"It wasn't always easy, though. The government made it that way. The people around us made it that way. Our love was deemed illegal. A law made by someone with hate in their heart hurt so many people who just wanted to live freely. Knowing that my children were born a crime still breaks my heart," she says. "People's skin color dictated their worth, and nothing else fills me with this kind of rage. I hope that every racist bastard who supported apartheid rots in hell." Ouma Lettie squeezes my hand. "We all deserve our happiness, regardless of our race, sexual orientation, or religion. No person on this earth has the right to take that away from us. I want you to always remember, Nate, you deserve to be who you are and love whom you love."

I squeeze her hand back. Ouma Lettie's words fill me with hope. Though Uncle Richard's words are still fresh in my mind, Ouma Lettie's are a balm to the soul. To know that I am loved and supported is healing.

I study Ouma Lettie. I can't begin to imagine all she had to go through to live the life she's had. I know that she has stories and scars. But she survived. She loved whom she loved and she was happy.

I want to be like that.

I will not let anything that happened last night ruin my time here. I refuse. I am going to enjoy being in South Africa with Ouma Lettie and Jai. I'll ignore everything else.

The sun rises. My spirits too.

27

It's the day before the wedding.

Jai and I spent the morning practicing "Run to You," and now we're with Ouma Lettie at a private game reserve. This is the wedding venue, owned by some billionaire friend of the family who lives overseas. All the guests will be staying here for a couple of nights. The three of us are among the first to arrive.

I said goodbye to the farm earlier today, which was harder than I thought it'd be. We'll spend the rest of our time here at the resort before we fly back home.

I can't believe my time in South Africa is already coming to an end. It's been an unforgettable two weeks—ups and downs included.

"Wow," Jai says. We walk into the resort's reception area and wait for our room assignments. "This is amazing."

The space is large. The walls are a crisp white, and hand-carved wooden furniture is scattered throughout. A tile mosaic on the floor is polished to a shine. Large floor-to-ceiling windows reveal the jungle outside. It's breathtaking.

"It's a waste of money is what it is," Ouma Lettie says. "I

keep telling these people it's not about how extravagant the wedding is but the quality of their relationship. Your grandfather and I got married just with a priest. It wasn't even legal for a few years." Ouma Lettie shakes her head. "Love doesn't need six zeroes."

"Just think of it as a holiday," I tell her. "Use this opportunity to relax." I feel closer to Ouma Lettie than I've ever felt.

"I could be doing so much work on the farm," Ouma Lettie says. "Is it really necessary to stay here for two nights?"

"I saw there was a spa—maybe you should book a massage or something?" I say. "It's nice to have people pamper you."

"No, thank you," Ouma Lettie says. "I don't like strangers touching me."

Jai laughs. "Me either. Massages aren't for me for that very reason."

"This way, please," the bellhop says. We follow her to our rooms. Ouma Lettie will be staying down the hall from us.

Jai opens the door to our room with his key card. The space is a decent size, with an en suite bathroom. There are two beds. I drop my luggage at the one closest to the door and head to the window to take in the view.

Wilderness spreads out below us. A herd of elephants trots in the distance. One picks at a tree with its trunk.

"Holy shit, Jai. Come see this." I turn to him excitedly.

Jai joins me at the window. He pulls out his phone and starts to record the elephants. We take a selfie with them to our backs.

"I look like crap," I say.

"You look fine," Jai says. "Now smile."

I do. Jai takes a few more pictures.

"Send them to me," I say. "Please."

"Sure," Jai says. "As soon as we get Wi-Fi again." We both read the sign in the lobby area—with its big, bold letters, it was kind of hard to miss. One of the features of this private game reserve is that it gives its guests the chance to completely disconnect from the world, and because of this ethos, there's no Wi-Fi. Which is fine and good for everyone else, but Jai and I currently don't have international roaming. We're two teenagers cut off from the internet for the weekend.

"I'll remind you about the photos when we get back home," I say, and throw myself onto my bed. The mattress is soft, and I let out a groan. The trip from the farm here was a few hours long.

Jai pulls out a pamphlet that he took from the lobby. "Oh, wow. The safari is open," Jai says. "We should totally go."

I sit. "Sure, when is it?"

"There's one at four p.m. The very last of the day."

I reach for my phone. Its only purpose now is to tell me the time. "We have an hour and a half to get there. Do we have to make a reservation?"

"Yeah. It says that it's included with the stay." Jai shrugs and scans the pamphlet for any more information.

"So it must be free for us, then?" I say.

"Only one way to find out." Jai picks up the phone and calls the lobby desk. When he's done with the call, he turns to me with a thumbs-up.

"I just booked the last two seats," Jai says.

"Lucky us." I stand up too. "We should go eat something first, though."

Jai nods. "Let's ask Ouma Lettie if she wants to join us."

We head for her room.

"We're going to try to get something to eat—do you want to come with us?" I ask Ouma Lettie when she opens the door.

"I have nothing better to do," Ouma Lettie says.

There was a map printed on a piece of paper in our room, so we follow Jai as he leads us to the reserve's restaurant.

"Jai and I managed to book seats on the last safari of the day," I tell Ouma Lettie. I didn't think I'd get the chance to experience something like that.

"You boys go ahead and have fun," Ouma Lettie says. "I went on one before. And that was enough for me."

We reach the reserve's restaurant, which serves food 24/7. It's buffet-style, so we each grab a plate and scan all the dishes. I take some meat, and salad too. I didn't plan on eating a lot, but as I look at all the food, I think that's about to change.

With our plates full, we move to an empty table. Jai carries Ouma Lettie's for her. I try not to swoon. Having served a large number of rude assholes at Big Mo's, I think a boy with manners is sexy.

After we've finished lunch and taken Ouma Lettie to her room, Jai and I go to the lobby, where we wait with a small group of people for our safari guide.

When I hold Jai's hand, a large man stares at us. He scowls. I try to move away from Jai, but he stops me and tightens his grip. Before I can say anything, the safari guide arrives. He's wearing all khaki, so he's impossible to miss.

"Hello," he says. "I am Johannes, and I will be your guide today." Johannes has an accent that I haven't heard this trip, but he'd probably say the same thing about Jai and me.

"The game reserve has not only the big five—lions, elephants, rhinos, leopards, and buffalo—but also many other animals. We will try to see most of them, but please remember that the animals are free to roam. So just because we are trying to see them doesn't mean that we will," Johannes explains as he leads us out of the lobby and toward a jeep.

"Also, remember to keep yourself and your limbs inside the vehicle at all times," he continues. "And please try to watch the noise level. We do not want to agitate any of the animals. Let's all have a safe and fun time."

"Well, that's reassuring," I whisper.

We pile into the jeep. Jai and I manage to score seating at the very back. The man who scowled at us sits two rows away. We take off. The roads are bumpy as we venture deeper into the wilderness. Our first encounter with the animals in the game reserve turns out to be the herd of elephants that Jai and I saw from our room.

The elephants are so close that I can see their wrinkly skin. I am in awe at just how large they are. They look like they could easily do damage to the jeep. And now my fascination is tinged by a little fear.

Next we see a herd of animals grazing. "These are impala," Johannes says. They scatter at the sound of our jeep. They are fast. I guess I would be too if I had to outrun hungry lions just to survive.

We enter a thicket of trees. A large branch scratches the top of the jeep. When we emerge, we are close to a watering hole. The lake glitters in the afternoon sun, and Johannes points out a herd of wildebeests lazing. The wildebeests are large and muscular, with heavy front ends, pronounced muzzles, and curved horns.

The jeep drives on. The road gets bumpier, and it has us all swaying in our seats. Jai grabs a handle to stabilize himself and throws an arm over my shoulder to do the same for me. When the rough patch of the road ends, Jai's arm remains. Not that I'm complaining. Instead, I lean into him.

We hear the lions before we see them. A pride of large tawny beasts lazes in the warm sun. A male lion stands and shakes his magnificent mane. He yawns, and we see his sharp teeth. This is the king of the jungle, and I do not want to get on his bad side.

"Relax," Jai whispers into my ear. "We're safe."

But even with his words, I only truly relax when we leave them behind. As we drive on, I rest my head on Jai's shoulder. The homophobic man turns to look at us again, shock in his eyes. This time I ignore him. I don't care about him, or about anyone else. Jai and I are doing what any couple would do.

The safari lasts an hour, and by the time we get back to the game reserve, the afternoon light has started to dim.

"It's good that we managed to get back before dark,"

Johannes says. "With the last safari ride it is always a worry. I hope you all had a fun time and made lots of memories."

We climb from the jeep, and as Jai and I walk, Mr. Homophobe leans over to talk to the woman next to him. She too turns to stare.

Out of spite for their judgment, I stop Jai and peck him on the lips. They look away quickly. That will surely give them something to talk about.

Jai laughs. "If you're going to kiss me, do it properly," he says. This time he kisses me.

And boy, oh boy, does he do it properly.

28

After the safari, Jai returns to our room, and I decide to explore the other facilities at the game reserve.

I hear him before I see him—Tommy.

He's just around the corner. As I get closer, I realize that he isn't alone. The voices get louder and more heated. Tommy and Erika are fighting.

"You've been like this ever since we got here," Erika says. "If you didn't want to be here, you shouldn't have come."

"Can you just stop, please?" Tommy says. "I'm going through some shit, and I don't need you constantly nitpicking at everything."

Erika sees me first. It would be too awkward for me to leave now. She storms off, bumping into Tommy's shoulder as she walks away. She doesn't look at me. I don't blame her. This wasn't for anyone to see, and I feel kind of bad for witnessing it.

Tommy turns to watch her leave—and he notices me. His face morphs from anger to confusion before he masks it completely with a detached expression. We stand like that for a while. Two boys with the burden of too much history between them, staring at each other.

Tommy makes the first move. He starts to carefully approach me, like I'm some scared animal that will flee at any sudden sound. I root myself in place. When he realizes that I'm not going anywhere, he eases into a stride.

"This is surprising," Tommy says. "You ran from me at the party."

I fold my arms across my chest. "Just because we spent one amicable morning together doesn't mean we're friendly," I say. "Shouldn't you chase after Erika?"

"I'm not in the mood to see her right now," Tommy says. He looks around. "Where's your boyfriend?" And his tone is almost mocking.

I stop myself from rolling my eyes. "I don't want to fight with you," I say.

Tommy exhales. "Me neither." And the way he says it reminds me of the Tommy I used to know. The Tommy I used to love a whole lot. I push back those memories. They are quicksand, and I refuse to be sucked in.

We fall into silence. And then Tommy breaks it.

"I've been wanting to talk to you," he says. "Ever since the tour."

"About what?" I ask.

Tommy shakes his head. "I thought I could just ignore it and act like nothing happened. Like I was your friend. But I can't. Spending time with you at the museums reminded me just how much I like hanging out with you." Tommy smiles, and it's the thing I fell for when I first saw him. A smile so wide it reveals all his teeth. I always liked being able to tell when he was really happy. "It didn't matter what we were doing. As long as we were together, I had a good time."

His words are innocent enough, but they send fire through my veins. They are the key to unlocking my anger.

I snort. "If you were going to miss me so much, why'd you dump—? Hell. No. Scratch that! You didn't even dump me— you just ghosted me. Stopped replying to my messages, stopped answering my calls. You even disappeared from social media. I had to figure out that I was being dumped all on my own."

I didn't plan on this outburst, but the angry hurt I've been wrestling with all this time rears its head. It's a beast. And a part of me doesn't want to lock these feelings away. I need to get this off my chest. It has been festering deep within me for too long. And it has taken a toll on me. How much? I didn't really realize until this very moment.

"It was the only way," Tommy says. "Was it the right thing to do? No, I know it wasn't. And I have regretted it every damn day since then. But it also felt like the only thing I could do to protect you."

"Protect me?" I ask. My voice is louder than before. "Are you hearing yourself? You broke my heart to protect me?"

"It's the truth," Tommy says. He runs his hands through his hair. "It's the only reason I'm in this stupid relationship with Erika." He shakes his head. "I've known I'm gay since I was thirteen years old. That hasn't changed."

"Why are you doing all this?" I ask. "What exactly are you protecting me from?"

"My father," Tommy says. He looks into my eyes, and I see

the fear inside him. Tommy and his father have always had a strained relationship. Mr. Herron expected too much from his son. He demanded perfection, regardless of the toll it took on Tommy. "He found out about me. About you. About us."

I stare at Tommy. And bit by bit, I piece together what he must have gone through.

"You know what my father is like," Tommy says. He sounds so sad when he speaks. I have to fight the urge to go to him and hug him. I even make a move toward him before coming to my senses.

Snap out of it, Nate!

"He said that if I didn't start living 'right,' he would make you pay," Tommy says. "I was just so scared that he would ruin either your life or your mom's. There's nothing he won't do to win. He's that type of person."

Mr. Herron is on the board at the hospital, and he is totally capable of ruining my mom's life.

"We're just teenagers," I say in disbelief.

"I am his only son. His pride and joy," Tommy says. "I can't be damaged in any way."

"You're not damaged," I say. "There is nothing wrong with you. At all." This is the power that parents have over their children. Their words and actions can scar. No gay person should ever be called damaged by anyone, especially by someone who should love them unconditionally.

Tommy is crying now. I've only ever seen Tommy in tears once during our relationship, and that was when he told me about his mother leaving him. He was six years old at the time.

Without thinking twice, I hug him. That to me is more

important than anything between us. I can't imagine what Tommy must have been going through. Being closeted is tough, but it's even harder when you realize that the closet is the only thing keeping you safe.

In this moment I hate Tommy's father more than I have ever hated anyone in my life.

Tommy bends to rest his forehead on my shoulder. I rub circles around his back. We stay like that until Tommy calms down.

"I miss you," Tommy says. His voice is rough from crying. He pulls back. I can see the redness in his eyes, the sadness.

"Tommy—I . . ." But I don't get to finish my thought, because he kisses me.

The touch of his lips catches me off guard, but it also brings me back. I see a supercut of our relationship—of all the good times. This is the first boy I ever loved. And at the time, I fully believed that my first love would be my last. I am a hopeless romantic.

When I come to my senses, I realize I am watching a train crash. I have to stop.

This is wrong.

This shouldn't be happening.

Nate, what the hell are you doing?!

No. No.

"No." I push Tommy away before I'm swallowed whole by my memories. I step back to create distance between Tommy and me. He's an open flame, and I'm in danger of getting burned.

"This isn't right," I whisper. I close my eyes to fight off whatever the hell I'm feeling. I do not want this.

Not with Tommy.

"Nate, I—"

I open my eyes when Tommy stops talking. He is no longer looking at me. He's looking over my shoulder at something else—at *someone* else. I turn to find Jai standing there.

Oh, God, did he see us kiss?

I get my answer when Jai turns on his heel and dashes away.

For a moment I am frozen in my spot, a living breathing statue. I can't do anything but stare as the boy I just hurt leaves.

I start to move after Jai, but Tommy grabs me. I fight him off and run. Jai is what matters now. I was a fool to give in to the past. I've ruined my future.

"Jai, wait!" I call out. "Please!" But he doesn't listen. He speeds up. Jai is faster than me, so he loses me in no time. I stop chasing after him. I fall on my knees, knowing how badly I screwed up.

I bury my face in my hands. This is not what I wanted. This is not how it was meant to be.

Fuck. Fuck. Fuck. Fuck.

I stand and run to our room. Jai has to come back eventually. I will wait for him for as long as I need to.

━━━━

Jai returns hours later. I'm sitting on the corner of my bed when he walks in. He doesn't look at me. And that hurts, so much.

"Jai, I'm sorry—" I start.

"I don't want to hear it, Nate," Jai says as he gets into bed.

"Let me explain, please," I say.

In response Jai simply switches off the lamp on his bedside table. None of this was supposed to happen. I'd hoped for closure with Tommy so that I could give my all to Jai. But I messed that up—*badly.*

It's apparent that the roads to both hell and heartbreak are paved with good intentions.

29

My current boyfriend saw me kissing my ex-boyfriend.

If what Jai was giving me before was considered the cold shoulder, the temperature now is subzero. And to make this whole situation even shittier, I don't blame him. Regardless of who started it, Tommy and I kissed. And Jai saw it.

I roll over expecting to find Jai in his bed, but he's already gone.

"Jai?" I call out, but he doesn't answer. I jump out of bed and go into the bathroom. It's empty. Jai isn't in the room.

I spend the morning looking for him, but he isn't at the restaurant for breakfast, and he isn't in any of the other places I look.

The pre-wedding buzz puts a stop to my search. All around, workers are putting last touches on what will be one of the biggest weddings South Africa will probably ever see.

Before it gets too late, I race back to my room and get dressed. Jai's suit is still hanging on the closet door. He hasn't returned yet, but he will come back if he wants to make the wedding. Then we'll be able to talk.

I sit on my bed, my leg nervously bouncing away. Every sound I hear outside the door sends my heart racing. Is that him? *No.* I get up to check the hallway a few times. When I can't sit anymore, I start to pace—from one end of the room to the other. Time stretches on, and soon I need to head down to the wedding venue.

I'll have to see him later, when he arrives at the reception. I have enough time to sort this out. Enough time to tell him just how sorry I am.

This is not how I wanted this week to be going. It was supposed to be an amazing experience for Jai and me, but it's all ruined. I was a bad boyfriend, and I was a terrible friend too.

I close my eyes and inhale a deep breath. I can fix this. I will fix it. I exhale and enter the venue. The wedding will take place on the massive deck that runs across the entire west side of the building.

White lawn chairs are spread out on either side of an aisle covered with white and red rose petals. The flower carpet leads up to a massive floral archway of the same colors. Ben, the pastor, and the best men are all standing there, waiting for the bride to arrive. They are framed by the game reserve's wilderness behind them.

Beyond the railing there are trees and grass and a massive lake. Guests hang out and take pictures of the many animals that call the reserve home. A herd of giraffes walks in the distance, zebras graze nearby, and hippos bathe in a lake. This is what paying top dollar will get you: a one-of-a-kind wedding.

And I can't really enjoy any of it, because my eyes are searching all the faces for Jai. I find Ouma Lettie seated on one of the chairs. She's wearing an understated emerald dress, and a headpiece crowns her gray hair. I make my way over to her and sit down.

"Where's Jai?" she asks. It's a question I would love to know the answer to myself. I shake my head. *I don't know.*

The rest of the guests begin to settle in, and I make sure to keep the seat next to me empty for Jai. Eventually a hush falls on us. The wedding is starting, and Jai is still missing. With a final scan of the crowd, I spot Tommy. He keeps staring at me, but I ignore him.

The bridesmaids enter. There are six of them. I recognize three—Brooke, Sasha, and Erika. The girls are wearing long red off-the-shoulder dresses. Each of them also carries a parasol covered with roses, alternating red and white flowers.

"The Wedding March" echoes, and we all rise to watch the bride make her trip down the aisle. Meghan glides in accompanied by Uncle Richard. There is a collective gasp when we see her. She looks breathtaking in a white gown with red lace accents that look like roses. The floral appliqué is spread across the front of the sheer bodice. The back is bare, and the accent detail continues down her very long train.

Uncle Richard beams next to her. I'm shaking hands with the idea that he'll never accept me. It isn't okay in the grand scheme of things—because homophobia in any way, shape, or form is never okay. But I will not allow him to have any power over me and the way I live my life. My happiness comes first.

I get swept up in the wedding, and by the time the ceremony is over, Jai still hasn't appeared. With the vows shared, we file into the reception hall. I extend my arm to Ouma Lettie so she doesn't get battered by the surging crowd.

The reception venue is filled with round tables covered with tablecloths that match the color scheme, and each boasts a number. Ouma Lettie and I stop before the seating chart.

"The writing is beautiful," Ouma Lettie says. "But so very small. I can't read a thing."

I scan the chart for our names. There we are: table 5. Henrietta Hargreaves. Nathan Hargreaves. Nathan Hargreaves Plus-One. We enter the hall and head over to our designated table.

The hall has been decorated with more flowers. Rows and rows of them hang overhead.

The wedding cake is set up by the dance floor. It has five tiers decorated with white and red roses.

Even though I'm starting to doubt that Jai will show up, I still look for him in the crowd.

Waitstaff weave through the crowd with drink orders. A waiter approaches our table. Ouma Lettie orders us something to drink, and by the time we finish the virgin cocktails, Meghan and her new husband have arrived.

Meghan has changed her outfit. Because why have only one wedding look when you can have two? I imagine that my cousin asked that very question. Meghan is not wearing a dress this time. Instead she's opted for a sleek white jumpsuit.

Even though I want to go and look for Jai, I stay and keep Ouma Lettie company. My hope is that Jai will turn up eventually. But hours later, he still hasn't appeared, and I excuse myself from the reception. On my way out, Tommy stops me.

"Can we talk?" Tommy asks. I've ignored him all along, which has been easy because Erika, who is clearly very tipsy at the moment, has kept him busy.

"No," I say. "I've said all I needed to say to you. We're done. I'm done."

"Nate, please," Tommy says. "Don't do this to me."

I spot Erika in the crowd. "Your girlfriend is looking for you," I tell him with a scowl. I jerk my arm free. Tommy calls after me, but I don't care. He isn't what's important right now.

Last time, Tommy Herron cut me out of his life. This time, I will be the one doing it. Our story is over. All I care about is the here and now. And here and now, I need to find Jai.

I race down the corridors. With the reception in full swing, the venue is all but deserted. Aunt Sylvia was serious when she said she'd booked the whole place for Meghan's wedding.

I reach our room and fumble for the key card. I shove it into the reader, and after a couple of tries the lock beeps. I push the door open to find an empty room. Not only is Jai missing, but his side of the room is completely empty—his luggage has disappeared too. It's like he was never here in the first place.

Jai is gone.

30

The only thing that Jai left behind is a letter—and me. The sheet of paper sits at the center of his bed—a page ripped from his notebook. I pick it up and read:

> Maybe it's childish of me to run away, but I just don't want to be here anymore. I want to go home. I asked your aunt for help changing my flight. I need time and space to think.

I reread the words over and over again, but the meaning doesn't change. He left. Half of me is angry at him for leaving me with nothing but the note. But the other half understands him. He agreed to be my plus-one for me. So of course he wouldn't stay here when I was making him upset. He doesn't owe me anything.

Hindsight really is twenty-twenty.

I ball the letter in my fist. This room is too quiet. I don't want to be here where Jai was supposed to be too. The empty side of the room is a reminder of all the mistakes I've made.

I head back to the reception. I grab a drink from a waiter and make my way out onto the deck. I take a sip and it's bitter—too bitter. It's perfect. I take another one. The alcohol burns going down. I lean against the railing and look out at the wilderness.

There's a roar off in the distance. Animals I can't see, their eyes glowing in the dark. A blanket of stars hangs overhead, yet I'm too miserable to enjoy it. I take one last sip of my drink and put the glass down. I'm flying out tomorrow night, and I don't want to travel with a hangover. I can't get drunk, even though I really want to.

Someone comes to stand next to me at the railing. I turn to find Tommy there. Tommy. Tommy. Tommy. Always damn Tommy.

"You're drinking," Tommy says.

"Good eye." I finish off the glass.

"Are you mad at me?" Tommy asks.

I exhale. "No." And it's the truth. I am not mad at Tommy. "I'm mad at myself. I messed up," I admit.

"You didn't," Tommy says. "This isn't how it's—"

I hold up a hand to silence him. We don't need to do this. And more important than that, I don't want to. Not anymore. I have the closure I was after. In the end it was more a me problem than a Tommy one. I needed to make a clean break from Tommy, and now I have. All that's left now is to say goodbye.

We stand in silence for a few heartbeats before Tommy breaks it. "I think I'll call you when we're back in the States," he says. "We can meet and talk then. I think that will be better."

I sigh. "No, don't," I say. "Don't call or text me. Don't bother.

We're through, Tommy. Completely. From now on you'll just be the boy I used to love, and that's it. It's over."

I walk away then.

This is enough.

It's all over now.

This is the last time that I will see him.

Goodbye, Tommy Herron.

I am not looking forward to the trip back home. I spend most of the day in bed, with no real reason to leave the room except to hunt for food. I have a late flight, so I use the excuse of wanting to sleep in preparation for the long trip. But in fact I've spent hours poring over Jai's letter.

I stare at my useless phone. I'm sure the reserve had good intentions when they thought up the no–Wi-Fi rule, but screw them. I need to text Jai. I won't be able to talk to him until I get back to Wychwood. How did people in the past reach their loved ones? Did they send a carrier pigeon? A letter in a bottle? Smoke signals?

When I close my eyes, I see the look on Jai's face after he saw me kissing Tommy. A knock at the door saves me from my misery spiral. I get out of the bed and look through the peephole: Ouma Lettie. I open the door.

"It's almost time for you to leave," she says. "Are you all packed?"

I nod. I dumped all my belongings into my luggage. I, the

neat freak, don't have the energy to pack with care. Mom would be shocked. In normal circumstances I would be too.

"Have you eaten something?" Ouma Lettie asks.

"Yeah," I say. "I had a late lunch."

Ouma Lettie doesn't ask about Jai, thankfully. I'm sure Aunt Sylvia told her he left. I collect my bag and head down to the lobby with Ouma Lettie in silence. I'm already emotional, but having to say goodbye to her now is about to push me over the edge.

"I'm going to miss you," I say.

She turns to me with a small smile. "Me too!" she says. "It was wonderful having you."

I hug her. "Thank you for everything."

"Of course," Ouma Lettie says. "You're my favorite grandson." I laugh even though I'm choked up. I'm her only grandson.

We break apart. This goodbye, unlike the one with Tommy, is bittersweet and not permanent. I promise to visit Ouma Lettie again. I want to spend as much time with her as I can before it's too late. I'm not sure how long she'll live, but I want as many memories of her as possible.

"Give my love to your mother," Ouma Lettie says. "And you keep being good. Don't give her any trouble."

"I'll make sure to call," I say. "A lot."

"Not too much, though. I have a social life to keep up with," Ouma Lettie teases.

I walk to the door, but I stop and run back to her. I hug her once more. God, *this is hard*. I don't want to cry, but I'm blinking back tears.

212

"You'd better go now before you miss your flight," Ouma Lettie says with a break in her voice.

I let go. "Bye."

This time Ouma Lettie follows. She waves me off. I get into the car that's waiting for me. As we drive away, I turn and watch Ouma Lettie. She's outside now, looking at me go. She's still waving. This time tears fall, and I let them.

I'll really, really miss you, Ouma Lettie!

The trip back home without Jai's company feels longer. I'm clearly being punished by the universe for messing up my relationship, because on the first flight I end up in a middle seat, sandwiched between a man with very long limbs who constantly steals my armrest and a kid with way too much energy. And on the second flight, we experience terrible turbulence. A clear sign that the universe has forsaken me.

Twenty-five long hours later, I touch down at LAX.

I am exhausted, physically, mentally, and emotionally.

But above all that, I miss Jai.

31

Mom is waiting for me at the airport when I arrive. In true Mom fashion, she even has a very large, very embarrassing sign with my name in bold, sparkling letters. I expect to find the glitter everywhere when I get home. At eleven years old I banned glitter after Mom used some to make me a costume for school. It literally got on everything.

"Sonno!" Mom shouts. She runs to me and hugs me tight. I melt into her embrace. Even though it's only been about two weeks, it feels so much longer.

"Hey, Mom," I say.

Mom studies me. "Glad to see you in one piece." I smile. My body may be in one piece, but my heart sure isn't. Mom looks over my shoulder. "Where's Jai?"

"He got an earlier flight." That's all I say. I start to pull my luggage.

"Why?" Mom asks.

"We had a fight," I say. "I don't really want to talk about it."

I follow Mom to the car. I can tell that she wants to ask me a thousand and one questions, but she's resisting the urge. And

I appreciate it. When we get into the car, she turns on the radio and I close my eyes.

I must doze off, because Mom's gentle taps startle me awake. "What is it?" I ask.

"We should eat something," Mom says. I look around, and we're in the parking lot at Big Mo's. I completely missed the ride home.

We go into the diner, where the familiar sounds, smells, and people greet me.

"I'm starved," Mom says as we sit down.

"You should have eaten something," I say. "It's way past lunchtime."

"I wanted to eat with you," Mom says.

I nod. "How's work been?" I immediately think of Mr. Herron. I only hope that asshole doesn't mess with Mom. I'd hate for her to suffer because Mr. Herron is horrible.

"Fine," Mom says. "Busy as always."

Lucille comes to get our orders. Mom and I both want a grilled mac and cheese sandwich—a family favorite. While we wait for our food, Mom gets coffee and I order a large Coke.

"Anything happen at home? Did you and Mr. Schuster get into it?" I ask, remembering that our video call ended with him knocking at the door.

Mom rolls her eyes. "That man, I swear," she says. "I try not to wish ill on anyone, but he really is testing me."

"Maybe we should move," I say.

"Nope. I refuse. We were here first. If anyone needs to leave, it's him," Mom says. "So anyway, tell me about your trip. How was the wedding?"

Our food comes as I'm telling Mom about my weeks in South Africa.

"I knew they would spend a pretty penny," Mom says. "But a private game reserve? Damn."

"It was amazing. I knew Aunt Sylvia and her friends were rich rich, but I didn't know just how rich *rich* until this trip."

"Seeing is believing," Mom says. She wipes at her mouth with a napkin. Mom is a faster eater than I am. She always has been. She gobbles her meals down. Whenever I call her out on it, she says it's a by-product of her job. Medical emergencies do not wait for things like meals.

Mom watches as I eat. And I know what she's thinking. We have skirted around the issue of Jai and me throughout the meal. But soon that's the only thing left to talk about. And knowing Mom, I'm sure we will need to.

"So you and Jai had a fight?" Mom prompts. She takes a sip of her coffee.

I nod.

"And it was big enough to make him leave early?" Mom asks.

I nod again.

"I did that once," Mom says. "Your dad and I went on a trip and ended up in a nasty argument. So I left him there. But I regretted it as soon as I calmed down."

"Really?" I ask. I wonder if maybe Jai regrets it too.

"Yeah," Mom says. "But it was also what I needed to do. I think if I'd stayed, the fight would have been worse. I had to leave. I needed that time and space or else we would've broken up again."

"Again?" I ask. "What do you mean?"

Mom chuckles. "Your dad and I argued all the time when we were dating," she says. "So of course we broke up a few times."

"You did?" I ask. This is the first time in a long time that Mom has spoken so freely about Dad. Maybe going to South Africa wasn't only good for me. Maybe it was good for her too.

"Of course. We were young and still trying to figure things out. That's a recipe for messiness." Mom takes another sip of her coffee. "Everything feels like do or die when you're young. Our actions. Emotions. Relationships. Even our mistakes. We shine our brightest when we're young, so it makes sense that our feelings burn like fire."

"I messed up, Mom," I say. "I understand why Jai's mad at me. And the worst thing is that I don't blame him for his reaction. He should be mad at me." Tears fill my eyes.

"Knowing and accepting that you messed up is the first step," Mom says. "We all do it. But not all of us are willing to take responsibility for our actions."

"What do I do? How do I fix this?" I ask.

"I'm not sure what it is that you did wrong," Mom says. "And you'll tell me about it when you're ready. But regardless of what it is, you have to apologize if you messed up. You say you're sorry and you try to do better."

"I'm going to, but what if that isn't enough?" I ask. I don't know if Jai will forgive me. A part of me isn't sure that if the roles were reversed, I would be willing to do so. And that is what scares me the most.

Mom reaches across the table and takes my hand in hers.

"Then you consider this a lesson learned," she says. "It'll be a hard one. One that will break your heart." She squeezes my hand. "The fact of the matter is that 'sorry' isn't enough sometimes. And you can't force it to be. But we're human, so we make mistakes. And because we're human, we can learn and grow from them."

I find comfort in Mom's words, even if she doesn't know all the details. Everything that Mom said is right. I *do* need to apologize. Whether Jai accepts it, only time will tell.

If he doesn't, I know that I will be devastated—utterly and completely heartbroken.

But I also know that in time I will heal.

And I will be better next time.

32

The first thing I do when I get home is plug in my phone so I can text Jai. It feels like it takes an hour for my phone to start up. Finally, it buzzes on.

I type, delete, and retype messages a thousand times, or at least it feels that way to me. How do I put all that I'm feeling, all that I'm sorry for, into a single message? It feels cold and impersonal. This isn't how I want to make amends. I want to see him face to face. I want to meet him as soon as possible. But what I want right now doesn't matter. This is the first step.

> I'm sorry, Jai. I want to apologize. Do you have time to meet? I know that I hurt you and you probably don't want to see me, but please, can we meet?

The message is delivered. But it's not read. A watched kettle never boils, Mom always says. So I force myself to put my phone down. I force myself to ignore it and do something else.

I move over to my luggage. I rip off the labels and stickers from my flights and open it. My clothes are a tangled mess. Dumping them in was not a great idea. I scold myself as I empty my bag.

Cry, the Beloved Country is buried under the pile of clothes. I asked Ouma Lettie for it before I left. She told me to take whatever I wanted. So I settled for the book and two photos, one of Mom and Dad and another of just him alone.

I place the book on my bedside table and then check my phone. The message still hasn't been read.

Give it time. Give him time, I tell myself. It becomes my mantra. I pin the two photos above my desk.

Mom pops her head into my room. "You should do laundry now," she says.

"Yeah, I was going to." With it just being the two of us, Mom and I have always been a team when it comes to house chores. I learned how to do laundry at a young age.

"What are you doing?" Mom asks when she sees me at my desk. She comes over to look.

"I got these from Ouma Lettie," I say, explaining the photos.

Mom stares at them in silence for a moment before reaching out and touching Dad's smiling face. "I miss him so much," Mom says. "We were so young here. He was so young."

"I'd love to hear about him, you know," I say. "Whenever you want to tell me."

Mom looks at the picture once more. She's smiling at the captured memory. "I think your dad and I had been dating for a year and a half when this was taken. We flew to South Africa for Aunt Sylvia and Uncle Richard's wedding. It was my first time visiting the country."

"Really?" I ask. "You were Dad's plus-one to the wedding?"

"Yeah. And the rest is history." She touches the photo one last time before leaving the room. South Africa has clearly been good to my family in the romance department.

I check my phone. Still nothing.

Give it time. Give him time.

I grab all my clothes and walk over to do the laundry. Once I throw in my first load, I join Mom on the couch. She's clicking through the channels.

"Aren't you tired?"

"A bit," I lie. The truth is, I am exhausted, but I want to wait and see if I get a response from Jai.

But I wait in vain, because my message is still unread, and soon I'm struggling just to keep my eyes open. I quickly shower and lose myself to sleep. My dreams are filled with Jai. With what-ifs that I hope can one day come true.

I sleep for longer than I intended to. My body is clearly unhappy about the different time zones. The first thing I do after blinking myself back to my senses is check my phone. This time my message has been read.

Finally! Relief floods my body. I wait to see if he's typing, but there's no activity.

Give it time. Give him time. Instead of calm and comfort, the mantra feels like salt to my wound. Will Jai and I be fine with time and space? I want to go over to his house, but I'm not sure if that will make matters worse.

I climb out of bed and head to the kitchen for some coffee. Mom's working today. What a great time to be alone with nothing to do but think and think and think.

I'm wallowing in misery and heartbreak when the intercom starts buzzing.

I walk up to the black box and press the talk button. "Who's this?"

"Honey, I'm home!"

"Gemma?" I ask.

"The one and only," she responds.

A couple of minutes later I open the front door and Gemma waltzes in. "You look like shit," she says, giving me the once-over.

"Gee, thanks," I say. I close the door and follow her into the living room. "Why are you here? You're supposed to be in LA."

"My internship was only two weeks, remember? I'm back home now, so I'm here to check on you," Gemma says as if it's the most obvious thing in the world.

"Check on me? Why?" How does Gemma know? I haven't told anyone, and I know that Mom hasn't either. There's only one other person. "Did Jai say something?"

"Yes," Gemma says.

"Well, what did he say?" I demand. I don't have time for games right now. I'm about to demand information, but Gemma holds up a silencing finger.

"Before you flip out, let's take a deep, calming breath. Okay?" Gemma says.

"I'm not going to flip out," I say defensively, even though I totally was. It seems we both knew it.

Gemma snorts. "Sure, let's say I believe you." She sits down, and I do too. I bite my tongue to stop myself from asking all the questions I have. Finally, Gemma starts talking.

"Jai and I spoke this morning," she says. "He mentioned that things weren't good between you two."

"I messed up," I say. "Tommy kissed me. And Jai saw it." I'm not looking at her when I say this.

"I know," Gemma says. "I can't believe you kissed the son of Satan."

"I didn't mean to. It just happened." I bury my face in my hands.

"Well, given just how screwed up your break—or lack thereof—was, I understand your mess of feelings. It's why I was happy Jai was there for you," Gemma says. She curses again. "I cannot believe I once shipped you and Tommy so hard."

"Do you think Jai hates me?" I look up at her. "Do you think I'm a bad person?"

"Of course not, Nate. We've been best friends since the time you thought crayons were a food group. I'll always be on your side," Gemma says. "And that's why I know Jai understands that you made a mistake. Forgiveness can take time. And he will move on, I'm sure of it."

"Really?" I ask. "You think so?"

Gemma nods.

"Thank you for being my best friend," I say, my voice trembling.

Gemma eyes me suspiciously. "Don't do it," she says. "I'm not wearing waterproof mascara."

I laugh because Gemma has this habit of crying whenever she sees someone else cry. I'm trying not to let my tears fall, but in the end I lose the battle, and Gemma does too. She fans herself.

"Sorry," I say.

"You should be," Gemma says. "I'm going to look like a raccoon."

"Call it fashion," I tease.

"You wouldn't know fashion if it bit you in the ass," Gemma says.

"Why does everyone keep saying that?" I ask. "My fashion sense is not that bad!"

Gemma stares at me. "You're joking, right?"

"I'm insulted. Don't kick a man when he's down," I say.

"And scene! Let's move past this and hear all about South Africa," Gemma says.

"Before that, do you want something to drink?" I ask.

"Whatever you're having is fine," Gemma says. I head to the kitchen and pour us both some juice.

She grabs the glass and takes a big sip. I do too. "My gentle weeping has made me thirsty."

"There was weeping, but it *wasn't* gentle," I say. I laugh and end up spitting out my drink.

I needed this. All the laughter and the teasing to distract me from the doom and gloom. But being with Gemma, I notice the obvious hole in our friendship. And it's in the shape of Jai. It's been the three of us for so long now.

Jai belongs here—with us.

With me.

33

Jai is still ignoring my texts, but I'm seeing him today. We have band practice at his house. And it'll be one of the most important ones. Not only are we playing our new song for the first time, but this will be my first attempt to fix what I broke between Jai and me.

I have been a nervous ball of energy all morning. I tried to distract myself by finishing *Cry, the Beloved Country*, but I just don't have the bandwidth right now. The only thing I can think of is that I will be seeing Jai in a few hours.

When reading fails, I try to watch TV but lose interest fast.

"Sonno, do you want a smoothie?" Mom shouts from the kitchen. She has the morning off. So she'll take me to Jai's before going to work.

"No thanks," I say as I continue to count down the minutes until band practice.

I change my outfit at least three times—and by "outfit," I mean my T-shirt. First from red to blue to green, unsure of which color says "Sorry." Anyone looking in would think that

I'm getting ready to go out on a date. This is me getting ready to try to win back the boy I like.

"Are you done?" Mom asks when I exit my room. There is no way I will be early now. Thank you, indecision. "That's the longest you've ever taken to get ready."

"I'm nervous, okay?" I turn to her with a frown on my face. "Was that a diss of my fashion sense?"

Mom studies me for a moment. "Yes."

I dash back into my room.

"What are you doing now?" Mom asks.

"I'm changing!" I say. I pull open my wardrobe once more.

"You look fine!" Mom says, but I don't believe her.

"You shouldn't have insulted my clothing in the first place," I say. "You reap what you sow!"

"Why are you so dramatic?" Mom asks. "And don't wear anything green. It's not your color."

A third of my clothes are in shades of green. I glare at Mom through the door. *You should have told me that before I went out and bought a whole wardrobe full of green clothes, dear mother.*

After another ten minutes of deliberating what to wear, I walk out with the very first shirt I tried on. Always trust your gut. I stop in front of Mom and do a slow turn. "Well?"

"You literally just changed a T-shirt—why did that take so long?" Mom says.

"That's not what's important right now. How do I look?"

Mom runs a hand through her hair. "Fine. You look great. You are just going to band practice. You are not getting married."

"That would probably be easier than getting Jai to forgive me," I say.

"You can do it," Mom says. "I believe in you."

"Thanks, Mom," I laugh. "Now, enough chit-chat—we're going to be late."

Mom looks at me in disbelief. The delay is clearly my fault.

The drive to Jai's is quicker than I hoped. Too soon I'm standing in his driveway. I've been so eager to be here, but now that I am, I feel more than a little scared. There is no guarantee that today will work out in my favor.

"You can do this, Nate." I exhale and walk toward the studio. I'm surprised to find Jai waiting at the door. I'm pretty sure that I am the last band member to arrive, so I wonder if maybe he is waiting for me. His face is an expressionless mask, telling me nothing.

What is going on?

"This competition is really important to me," Jai says. "Can we just focus on that, please? I really don't have the energy for anything else." With that out of the way, he turns around and walks into the studio.

This is going to be every bit as hard as I thought it would be. I try not to let his words discourage me. Jai can say that. Hell, he can say so much more. I deserve it.

Inside, everyone turns to me when I walk into the rehearsal space—everyone but Jai, that is.

"Sorry I'm late," I say.

We have just a week to learn a completely new song. And

because of this, our first run-through is a disaster. Liam starts a beat later than he should. Simon misses his cue too. And my voice cracks on one of the high notes.

At the end of the rehearsal, Jai gives us a speech.

"We'll get better," he says. "We just need more practice."

Everyone starts to leave, but I hang around in the hopes of getting a chance to talk to Jai again. Farrah comes in and signals me to follow her, which I do, nervously. She must be mad at me if she knows what I've done. Blood is thicker than water.

We enter the main house through the back door. The Patels' kitchen is large and modern, with light-toned wooden cupboards and white marble countertops. There's a big island in the center. Farrah opens the large stainless-steel fridge. "Do you want something to drink?"

"No thanks," I say.

Farrah grabs a bottle of water. "I didn't mean to eavesdrop, but I heard my brother talking to Gemma about what happened between you two," Farrah says.

"So you know what I did?" I ask. "I suck. I'm sorry."

"I'm not judging you," Farrah says. "Emotions are weird, and relationships are even worse."

"I messed up. I know I did. I keep trying to apologize for it."

"Don't give up," Farrah says. "I like you and my brother as a couple. I want you to get back together, but I also want you to know that it probably won't be easy. Jai's been hurt like this before."

"He has?" I ask. Jai has never told me about his past relationships. I know he's dated other people but not the details.

"Yeah. Before we moved here, there was a girl Jai really liked," Farrah says. "They dated, and everything was going well for them. But then one day Jai saw her with her ex-boyfriend. She left Jai for her ex."

The story reminds me of me and Tommy. But the difference is that I don't have any intention of getting back with Tommy. The past is the past for a reason. Yes, I had a momentary lapse in judgment, but that's all it was—nothing more. I regretted it immediately after. I don't want those five seconds of stupidity to be the death of our relationship. I'm certain that I don't want to be with Tommy. I want to be with Jai. I know that now more than ever.

"He's dated other people on and off, but no one came close to what he felt for her," Farrah says. "That is, until you." She smiles sadly. "He really likes you. And I think that's why he's acting this way."

"I really like him too," I say. "And I don't want to lose him."

"Then you need to show him that," Farrah says. "Right now he's doubting your relationship. You need to fix that."

I agree. And I will.

I will win Jai back.

Our love story hasn't ended yet. It's just beginning.

I return to the studio. Jai is still there. He sees me but turns his back to me.

"You don't need to say anything," I tell him. "Just listen." I close the studio door behind me, and he looks at me. "I'm sorry," I say. "More than you'll ever know. I messed up. I'll regret what happened forever. But I want you to know that I'm not giving up on us." I pause before continuing, "I like you a lot, Jai. More than I even realized, if I'm being honest with you. Maybe I even love you. I don't know. Either way, I want to find out with you." I take a step toward him but stop. I'll only talk today. "I'm going to win you back, Jai Patel." And with that I leave.

My heart is pounding in my chest and my palms are sweaty. I lean against the outside wall of the studio and exhale a nervous breath. I pull out my phone and text Mom to tell her that practice is over. I don't get a response from her, so after a few minutes I try to call, but there isn't an answer. There must be an emergency at the hospital.

I'm still standing there when Jai exits the studio fifteen minutes later. He looks surprised to see me here.

"I promise that I'm not staying here on purpose," I say. "Mom's not picking up."

Jai stares at me for a moment. I fidget with my shirt. I'm about to ask him if something's wrong when he speaks.

"Come on," Jai says. "I'll give you a ride home."

"Really?" I can't hide the shock in my voice, and a smile crosses Jai's face. It's a small one, but at least it's something.

"Yes, really," Jai says.

I follow him to his car and get into the passenger seat.

"This doesn't mean anything," Jai says as he starts the car.

"Of course," I say.

"I'm serious, Nate," Jai says, and I grin. I can't help it. Jai is actually talking to me. He looks very confused. "Why are you smiling?" he asks.

"I just missed you saying my name is all," I say.

Our eyes meet, and Jai looks away. He clears his throat nervously and starts to drive.

It may be difficult for us to get back to where we were, but I know that it will be worth it when we do.

Jai and I belong together.

I just need to remind him of that.

34

Jai drops me off at home, and I see him drive into the night. I can't fight the grin on my face. Even though we rode over in silence, I still caught him sneaking looks at me a few times. Those small glances are enough to give me hope—like raindrops in a desert.

I walk inside. As I'm waiting for the elevator, my phone vibrates with a call from Mom.

"Hey, Mom," I say.

"Hey, Sonno! Sorry, there was a massive accident on the highway, so it was all hands on deck."

"No worries," I say. "Jai gave me a ride home."

"He did?" Mom asks. She sounds as excited as I am. "Did you guys get to talk?"

"Not really," I say. The elevator arrives and I get in. "But I'm not giving up."

"That's the spirit," Mom says. "But you know, if all my rom-com watching has taught me anything, it's that you can't go wrong with a grand gesture."

"A grand gesture?"

"Yeah," Mom says. "Just a second." I listen as Mom's name is called over the intercom. "I have to go, Sonno! I'll see you later. Love you!"

By the time the doors open on my floor, the first sparks of an idea are flying in my head. If I need a romantic grand gesture, then that's exactly what I'll do.

———

The next day Gemma and I have a shift at Big Mo's. It's been a busy morning. There are all the kids who are still on vacation, plus a bunch of locals and visitors. But I find Gemma during a brief lull in our shift.

"Can you do me a favor?" I ask her.

"What do you need?" Gemma asks.

"Can you text Jai and ask him to come here?" I say.

"Why?" Gemma asks.

"Well, we have band practice today. And I'm thinking if he comes now, he'll offer to give me a ride. Which means I get to spend time alone with him," I say.

"What are you cooking up, Nathan Hargreaves?"

I lean in close and whisper.

After a moment, Gemma smiles. "I love a well-thought-out plan." She gives me an okay hand sign.

Just after the lunch rush, the bell above the door announces Jai's entrance. I'm pouring some customers' coffee when I see him. It's about time for my shift to end. My plan has worked. I watch him as he walks over to a table. He's careful not to sit in my area, but I don't mind. I'm just happy that he's here.

I pull Gemma aside when she walks by with an empty tray. "You texted him?" I ask.

"Uh . . ." Gemma looks guilty. "I was going to, but then we got that big wave of customers and I forgot. Sorry."

"But he's here," I whisper. I've asked if I can leave early for band practice, but Gemma is still in her uniform working.

"I know," Gemma states. "I can see that."

If this isn't my plan in action, why is Jai here? I mean, he's free to come and go as he pleases, but the timing is odd. And I don't believe in coincidences.

"Hey," Gemma greets him.

"Hey," Jai replies. Then he turns to look at me. "I can give you a ride to practice," he says. "If you want."

"Is that why you're here?" I ask.

Jai shrugs, not really giving an answer. Either way, I nod. This is what I planned and hoped would happen, and yet I played no part in making it happen. We say goodbye to Gemma and head outside.

"Thanks for the ride," I say when we're in his car and on the way to his house.

"We're still friends," Jai says. I don't let his attempt to friend-zone me get to me. I don't want to be just friends. And I've been working on something to win him back.

Jai is starting to let his guard down. We now talk to each other and have even exchanged a text or two. It looks like we are well on our way to being friends again. Two days before Ready2Rock, I am finally prepared to deliver my big rom-com moment. Which is why I am standing outside Jai's house.

I text Farrah. I asked her for a favor, and she's been more than willing to help. She replies, telling me that the studio door is unlocked and that she'll be sending Jai down soon. I promised her a meal when this is all over.

I sit behind the keyboard. That is where Jai finds me when he enters the room.

"Nate, what are you doing here?" he asks. "We don't have practice today."

I know that. I wanted it to be just the two of us.

This scene is a carbon copy of the day Jai and I met—me seated at the piano and him watching from the doorway. Looking back now, I'm one hundred percent certain that I fell for him then. I had too much going on at the time to realize it, but my heart is sure it's been love all along.

Instead of answering Jai's question, I start to play him a love song. My fingers dance across the keys. This ballad is my grand gesture. I've spent all week working on it. I've always written songs whenever I've needed to work stuff out, so why not a performance to tell Jai just how much I care about him? Not as a friend but as my boyfriend.

"*We were always going to collide / It was chemistry / Like we were meant to be . . .*," I begin to sing. Jai looks confused at first, but he's listening to my song. Or rather, he is listening to *his* song. It's even called "For Jai."

My eyes are closed as I enter the chorus.

"This simple song is for you, my love / I'll sing it a thousand times to you, my love / In my heart there's only you, my love / I'll do it all for you."

When I open my eyes to deliver the next part of the song, I see Jai staring at me. Our eyes stay connected as I play. I stop thinking and just let the music flow out from me. I pour everything that I'm feeling right now—and everything that I feel for Jai too—into the song.

I'm on the verge of tears when I deliver the last line of the chorus. *"I'll do it all for you."*

We're still staring at each other when I lift my fingers off the keyboard. I'm breathing heavily. I've bared my heart, and I can only hope that Jai is willing to see that.

I can only hope that his heart was listening too.

Jai clears his throat. "You wrote that?"

I'm unable to speak, so I nod.

"For me?" he asks.

I nod again.

The silence stretches between us. I'm still seated at the keyboard, and Jai's standing there. I'm not sure what he's thinking or feeling.

Time seems to slow down as Jai closes the distance between us. Before I know it, Jai grabs my face in his hands and leans over the keyboard to kiss me. I'm too shocked to react at first, but then I lean into the kiss.

We kiss until we're both breathless. When we pull back, I say, "I've missed you."

"Me too," Jai says, misty-eyed.

I stand and walk around the keyboard. I bury my face in his chest and take in his smell.

"I really, really love you. You know?" I say.

Jai chuckles. "That's good, because I really, really love you too."

We kiss again, and as we do, I pull Jai tight against me. My hands trace his broad back, and he runs his hands through my hair. Jai's arms feel like home.

I never want this moment to end.

And it doesn't for a long time.

35

The day of Ready2Rock arrives, and even though I am nervous, I am happy too. I have been floating on cloud nine ever since Jai and I kissed, and nothing can bring me down. I roll over in bed and yawn. Jai and I stayed up most of the night talking.

Mom pops her head into my room. "I'm going to be leaving soon," she announces. "You and Jai be safe out there. Text or call if anything happens."

"I will, Mom," I promise.

"Love you," Mom says. I hear her leave the house. That she has already left for work means that I need to get out of bed and get moving. I jump off the bed and run to the kitchen.

Still in my boxers, I pour a bowl of cereal. I'm too nervous to eat anything heavier than this. My phone vibrates with a text from Gemma wishing us luck. I shower after breakfast and begin getting dressed in my room.

My outfit for the performance is hanging on my closet door. Gemma designed costumes for the band so that we all look cohesive. We settled on a black-and-red color scheme. I pull on the black ripped jeans and black-and-red-striped T-shirt. As I'm tying my shoes—combat boots—I get a text from Jai telling me that he's waiting in the parking lot.

My building is the closest to the highway, so I am the last band member to be picked up. I'm surprised to find that the front passenger seat is empty, though. Not that I'm complaining. And I'm definitely not complaining about the peck Jai gives me when I climb on board.

"Ooh la la," Liam teases.

"Enough with the lovey-dovey," Simon says.

"Don't be jealous, Si," Raquel says.

Jai and I laugh. The drive to LA feels short. And when we arrive at the venue, we all stay seated in the car for a while.

"So are we just going to stay here or what?" Simon asks.

"We're just taking a minute, Simon," Raquel says. For the first time ever, she sounds nervous.

"We can do this, right?" Liam asks.

"We can do this," Jai says. "We've wanted this for a long time. A chance to share our music."

We all nod and get out of the car. We collect our equipment and stare at the venue, which has already started filling up. The organizers rented an entire park and built a stage. Ready2Rock is so much bigger and more elaborate than I thought it would be. Which is very good for the band but very bad for me and my stage fright.

We head backstage to check in. There are other bands there, and we're split into two separate groups in the waiting area. We find a spot for ourselves and get settled in for the contest to start.

The lights go up and the crowd starts cheering. Ezra Grace from the Graces steps onto the stage looking every inch the rock star that he is, and the crowd loses their shit. Ezra Grace is wearing a full denim ensemble. On anyone else it might look dated and out of fashion, but on him it looks just right. That must be the power of a superstar—or a great stylist.

This is the first time in my life I'm seeing a celebrity up close and personal, so I can't help but stare.

"Quit gawking or I'm going to get jealous," Jai whispers into my ear.

I turn to him. "You're the only rock star for me."

"Thank you all for coming," Ezra Grace says. "I'm so happy to be a part of Ready2Rock. I'm excited to find the next generation of rock musicians. To the contestants, give your all and leave everything on the stage. But remember to enjoy this moment. This performance is as much for you as it is for the crowd. I wish you all good luck." He turns to the crowd and shouts, "And I hope you're all Ready2Rock!"

The Graces start to play their new song, which is already topping the charts and getting a lot of airplay. They're well on their way to becoming pop-rock royalty. We all watch as Ezra Grace and his band set the stage on fire. God, if we only perform half as well as they do, we'll win.

When the set ends, Ezra heads for his seat among the judging panel. This is it. The competition will be starting soon. The host heads out onstage to introduce the first band.

We were all emailed the lineup last night. We're performing in the middle of the pack. Two slots after Ross and Thorn, whom we haven't seen yet. They must be in the other waiting area. Which is a good thing, because we don't need that asshole messing with our heads. We need to focus.

We hear the performances from backstage. Each one is better than the last. The competition is tough.

"All right, all right," says the host as Thorn, and Ross, take the stage. While the band sets up, Ross scans the backstage area. I feel the moment his eyes land on his old band—and on Jai. He smirks and winks, the picture of arrogance. I take Jai's hand in mine, interlocking our fingers.

Thorn starts to perform the first of their three songs. And they start with "Alone," the song that Infinite Sorrow was supposed to perform today. From the first chord the crowd goes wild.

We watch, and I hate to admit it, but Thorn is doing really well. Until they reach the chorus, when Ross messes up one of his lyrics. I don't mean to revel in someone else's failure, but I can't exactly say that I feel all that sorry for him. A saint I am not. I look over at Jai, and he is beaming too. We are clearly of one mind on this matter. What goes around comes around.

Thorn finishes off their set, but we ignore them when they walk past us. They're not what's important right now. Nothing else matters but our band.

The last band before it's our turn to perform is called onto the stage. We watch their first two songs, but during their third Jai calls us over.

"Let's have fun," Jai says. "This is a once-in-a-lifetime opportunity, so let's make the most of it. If we leave all we've got on the stage, it doesn't matter if we lose or win."

Jai holds his hand out, and we all pile ours on top. Of course, I've made sure that my hand is the one on Jai's.

"Let's do this!" Raquel says. Her eyes are alight with determination. I see the same look on everyone else's face. We all want to perform, and we all want to do it well.

"Yeah," we all say as we throw our hands up. When the other band finishes their set, the host heads to the stage to introduce us.

"Next we have a prominent favorite on the indie scene, a band that is sure to get every single one of you on your feet dancing. Let's all welcome Infinite Sorrow."

The crowd screams for us. One by one we head out there. I take my place behind the central microphone and watch as the rest of the band gets set up.

I feel like I'm going to throw up, but Jai walks over to me. "It's just like that night in South Africa, remember?" Jai says. "I'm right here with you. We can do this."

I nod. "Just like South Africa." I can do this. I *will* do it. My stage fright will not hold me back today. I exhale. Liam counts us in with his drumsticks.

We start with "Antihero." The crowd clearly loves the song as much as I do. "Antihero" can be considered trademark Infinite Sorrow. I lose myself to the live music around me and the many screams and shouts from the crowd. As soon as "Antihero" ends, we go straight into "Shadow," another well-known song in our catalog.

Jai has decided that we should close our set of three with our new music. We all trust him and agree. I'm more nervous than I was before. This is the song Jai and I wrote, so it holds a special place in my heart. I'm both excited and more than a little nervous to find out how the crowd reacts to it.

The first chords of "Run to You" start playing, and I deliver the opening line. I still can't believe Jai and I managed to write it. The song builds and builds, picking up pace until I am forced to flex my vocal cords.

Jai sings backup vocals throughout. Everything is just as we practiced. No one would be able to tell that we've only been playing this song as a band for a week. I'm so proud of us. We faced a crisis and overcame it. I may have been a last-minute addition to the band, but right now I am as much a part of Infinite Sorrow as everyone else. Right here, right now, we are one.

As we hit the chorus of the song the second time, I feel that the crowd is with us. They love this song as much as we do. That encourages me to let loose.

And just like Jai said, winning or losing doesn't matter. Not in this moment. What it's about is being here, on this stage, with the crowd screaming and our band playing. What matters is that our hearts are full of music.

I look to my left and see Jai playing the guitar. He meets my eyes.

What matters most is that I am here with the boy I love.

And there is no one else I'd rather be with.

Run

When it gets dark out, and I'm alone
I hope to find a place like home
This lost little boy only dreams of escaping
But my demons won't let me
They linger on
This lost little boy only dreams of escaping

I want to run, get away faster than you can catch me
I want to run, far away where no one can tame me
Run, run (run away)
Live my life on the run
I'm chasing my dreams and no one can stop me
So I'll run

My heart is tired, my soul is weak
I need some peace, I need some silence
I just want to escape
But your words are chains, and my hope is fragile
My feet are lead
(I'm not going anywhere)
There's just too much going on in my head

I want to run, get away faster than you can catch me
I want to run, far away where no one can tame me

Run, run (run away)
Live my life on the run
I'm chasing my dreams and no one can stop me
So I'll run

If I run, run (run away)
Will you even miss me?
If I run, run (run away)
Will you try to find me?
I'm gonna run, run (run away), live my life on the run
So watch me chase the sun . . .

I want to run, get away faster than you can catch me
I want to run, far away where no one can tame me
Run, run (run away)
Live my life on the run
I'm chasing my dreams and no one can stop me
Now watch me chase the sun
Just watch me chase the sun

Run to You

It starts so suddenly, as I'm looking at you
I remember us talking, but you don't have a clue
My feelings are growing, my longing is showing
I'm thinking about you
I'm thinking about you
(Only you)

So, please don't crush this crush of mine
Please don't make me lose my mind
(Can you give me some time?)
So, please don't crush this crush of mine
Please don't break this heart of mine
(Can you give me a sign?)
All I want to do is run to you

My heart is racing, I'm done pacing
This is my chance, I'm gonna take it
My nerves are steel, I'll tell you how I feel
This is my confession, will you listen?
(I think . . . uh . . . I really like you)

So, please don't crush this crush of mine
Please don't make me lose my mind
(Can you give me some time?)

So, please don't crush this crush of mine
Please don't break this heart of mine
(Can you give me a sign?)
All I want to do is run to you

You're the sun, and I'm the earth
I keep revolving around you
I'm the ocean, and you're the shore
I keep breaking for you
There's all this confusion
There's all this emotion

So, please don't crush this crush of mine
Please don't make me lose my mind
(Can you give me some time?)
So, please don't crush this crush of mine
Please don't break this heart of mine
(Can you give me a sign?)
I'm gonna run to you
I'm gonna run to you

Acknowledgments

Writing a book is hard. Writing a second book during a global pandemic felt like a mission impossible. And I would not have been able to do it without the help of many wonderful individuals.

First, I'd like to thank my family: Dad, Mom, Granny, Shane, Charne, and the three little ones who fill my days with joy. Having you in my corner makes a world of difference. Your love and belief are irreplaceable. I love you!

To Naadira, we've been friends for close to a decade now, and I'm very glad to know you. To Tammy, Allan, and Darren, thank you for always being my pillars of support. I really lucked out in the friend department.

Alexa Donne, friend and part-time mentor, thank you for the advice. You're a gem.

To my amazing editor, Polo Orozco, thank you for being the perfect partner for this book. I know that without you, *Nate Plus One* would not be the book it is today, and I'm grateful for every note that pushed me to tell a story I love and am proud of. A special thank-you to Tricia Lin for coming on board and helping me get across the finish line. I'm so very grateful!

A massive thank-you to the rest of the Random House team: Regina Flath, Alison Impey, Andrea Lau, Janet Foley, Barbara Bakowski, Alison Kolani, Jonathan Morris, and Caitlin Whalen. Thank you for the hard work you've put into *Nate Plus One*.

Barbara Marcus, Mallory Loehr, and Michelle Nagler, you have my gratitude as well.

Thank you to Kingsley Nebechi for the amazing cover art and for giving my book such a pretty face.

Thank you to Sahrish for your insights on Jai and his family. I greatly appreciate your time and effort.

Thank you to my agent, Robert Guinsler. Being a writer can be tough, but with you by my side, always offering your ear and having my back, it feels so much easier. You are the best agent I could ask for.

To the rest of Sterling Lord Literistic Inc., thank you for your support. Special thanks to Christopher Combemale.

Last but certainly not least, I thank you, dear reader, for picking up my book. I hope you've enjoyed your trip with Nate and Jai.

31901068247743